Murder on Castaway Island

Alicia Gael

Murder on Castaway Island

Alicia Gael

BELLA
BOOKS

2024

Dedication

To my first-grade teacher, Mrs. Thompson, who taught me how to read and write.

A million times, thank you.

Glossary of Characters

Guests:

Catherine Ames	Overly religious spinster
Darcy McDonald	Retired psychology professor and researcher
Emery Brennan	Medical doctor
Joan Hathorne	Retired judge
Phyllis "Phyl" Long	Ghostwriter
Rosie Roberts	Housekeeper, married to Theo Roberts
Tamara Miller	Wealthy party girl
Theo Roberts	Nonbinary butler, married to Rosie Roberts
Virginia "Virgie" Campbell	Unemployed educator
Wilma "Willie" Kerrel	Retired cop, now a private investigator

Others:

Frankie Nugent	Operates the boat to and from Castaway Island

CHAPTER ONE

Friday, Just before Noon

Sitting alone on the ferry, she knew the others were nearby. A smile played across her face as she looked out the grimy window at the choppy blue-green water. The day of reckoning was at hand. The plan had fallen into place as easily as pieces of a child's jigsaw puzzle. She and the others would be assembled on the island by five o'clock. All of them had accepted their invitations or offers of employment. She chuckled to herself. Greed and desperation made for easy marks.

She crossed her legs, glanced around the cabin, and located six invitees. She narrowed her eyes and gazed from one to another, her foot bobbing up and down. She fumed silently; they had gotten away with their transgressions for far too long. They needed to be held accountable. The dead deserved justice—they deserved retribution. She would make sure they got it. All nine would pay with a pound of their flesh. An eye for an eye. She would take the sword of Themis, the goddess of justice, into her hand and punish them herself, sending a warning to others: if you took a life, you would reap the consequences.

Tamara Miller sped down Highway Three, going twenty miles over the posted limit. She passed cars with the thinnest of margins, zipping back in line at the last second, her sun-bleached blond hair blowing wildly in her wake. She lived on the edge; she loved speed and wasn't afraid to take risks. No boring life for her. And with her daddy's money, she had the means to get the adrenaline high she craved. *Life's too short to be boring.* It was a motto she lived by.

She had spent the past week in Provincetown, surrounded by beautiful women wearing bikinis in every size, style, and color. She was a regular on the lesbian East Coast party circuit. When she'd received the engraved invitation at her Upper East Side Manhattan flat from a sorority sister she couldn't remember, who invited her to a weekend blowout on a private island, she jumped at the chance. She'd heard of Castaway Island and knew that movie star Grace Taylor had owned it until recently. *Too bad it still wasn't hers. Those Hollywood people knew how to party.*

She passed the car in front of her and almost missed the entrance to the ferry building. She pulled into the parking lot and took up two spaces. *Let them give me a ticket.* She wasn't taking any chances that her beautiful red Corvette would get dinged.

As Tamara stepped out of the car, heads turned to look at her, and she relished the attention of both sexes. She stretched, and fluffed her hair, flashing a smile at the two young women who looked at her with interest. Tall and well-proportioned, she paid her fitness trainer a pretty penny to keep her toned and shapely. She didn't give a fig about the men who stopped and stared at her as if she were a goddess put on Earth for their pleasure. Chuckling, she flashed them a well-practiced fake smile and silently laughed at the men ogling her.

She positioned herself for a photo op with the ferry behind her, pulled out her phone, snapped a selfie, and sent it to her half-million Insta followers. Life was good if you were Tamara Miller.

Doctor Emery Brennan was exhausted. Success had its drawbacks—lack of sleep was one. But it also had its rewards, such as the hundred-thousand-dollar Lincoln Navigator she currently drove. Although she could own something sleek and sporty that turned heads, she preferred the size and weight of the black SUV. It was a fortress, a layer of protection.

Today, she left her Boston medical office at noon and was headed south on Highway Three. Letting her shoulders relax, she lowered the windows and filled her lungs with fresh Atlantic air, not caring that the wind played havoc with her short, sandy-blond hair. The ninety-minute drive gave her time to reflect on her career and how she'd ended up at the top of her profession by the age of forty. Of course, skill played a part, but she'd also been lucky that the right patient had walked into her office at just the right time, and lucky she'd recognized the little-known, little-understood condition the woman suffered from, and even luckier the woman was married to a well-known politician. Saving the woman's life generated a lot of attention and appreciation from the woman's husband, a well-connected East Coast senator. Her reputation had skyrocketed. She became the doctor women clamored to for treatment of "women's issues."

She'd become very successful, but it had taken its toll. Although her practice thrived, she had little time for herself. She hadn't been on a date in over a year and couldn't remember the last time she'd had sex. Her last vacation was to an unmemorable medical convention in Denver over five years ago.

She leaned back against the headrest and thought about the certified letter from Mr. Knowles. He'd asked her to come to his home on Castaway Island—all expenses paid—to treat his wife's mysterious medical condition. Enclosed was a check for ten thousand dollars and a ticket for the afternoon ferry on September sixteenth. Curiosity won out. She was throwing caution to the wind and heading to Hyannis to catch the afternoon ferry to Nantucket. It wasn't exactly a vacation, but a few days on a private island would be a welcome break.

As she flipped the turn signal to enter the ferry building's parking lot, an ear-splitting blast from a car horn cut through the quiet morning. A young blond woman behind the wheel of a souped-up blue BMW cut in front of her from the opposite direction and raced into the parking lot ahead of her. "Fucking idiot!" she yelled out the window. Emery hated people who took unreasonable risks and didn't appreciate how fragile life was. She knew all too well that one wrong move, one blink, and it could all be gone.

Retired Professor Darcy McDonald gazed out the window of the Nantucket-bound ferry at the blue-gray ocean. Ferries were a damn slow way to travel, in her opinion. They were inefficient and uncomfortable to boot. Nantucket was only thirty-two miles south of Hyannis Port, but it would take at least another hour to arrive at the rate they were going. Then she had to take another boat to Castaway Island. She hoped those seats were padded. The plastic benches on the ferry were hard as a rock. Looking at her reflection in the salt-stained window, she noticed a few new wrinkles on her forehead. Surprisingly, only a few strands of gray invaded her shoulder-length black hair. She wondered if she should color it once it became more noticeable. Silently, she laughed at herself and shook her head. No, she'd let it turn gray. Plenty of sexy women had gray hair. It wouldn't be the end of the world.

She looked out across the water and blue skies and reached into her jacket pocket, pulled out her phone, and read the emailed invitation from someone named Knolles.

"*... a few of the men and women from NYU are reuniting and would love to see you there to reminisce and share stories.*"

As she refolded the paper and returned it to her pocket, she wondered about the sender. She was baffled, unable to remember anyone named Knolles at the university. The person must be a friend of her colleagues Tiger Gibson or Tammy Robertson.

She closed her eyes and leaned back as the ferry continued its journey. It would be good to see them again. She hadn't heard from her colleagues since she'd retired five years ago. She assumed no one knew what to say after what happened to Robby, her graduate student, and the death of her husband the following year. She let out a breath, relaxed her shoulders and stretched her neck from side to side. No matter. The past was the past. They had reached out now and wanted to reconnect. That was something.

At 12:01 p.m., sixty-year-old Catherine Ames sat on the hard plastic bench of the steamship to Nantucket, her back as straight as a board. She drummed an index finger on her well-worn black Bible that rested in her lap. *Why isn't the ferry leaving?* She made a tsking sound with her tongue as a couple rushed up the gangway. *Why don't people care about being on time?* It was a character flaw, one she despised. Keeping to a schedule was ingrained in her by her father, who'd been a colonel in the Army before becoming the pastor of his own church. She was responsible and always on time. People today were soft and undisciplined. They were hedonists and heathens, only caring about their own pleasure and beauty. She shook her head; they were sinners. They whitened their teeth, injected Botox into their faces, and had fat sucked out of their rear ends and injected into their lips. And the clothes they wore, especially the women…half-naked, just asking for trouble. She ground her teeth and made a tsking noise again. Indeed, God would hold them accountable.

She opened her Bible and took out the handwritten note. She appreciated that someone else took the time and effort to pen a letter; most people were too lazy to care about such things and sent impersonal emails.

She took the letter out of the envelope and read:

Dear Miss Ames,

I hope you remember me from the Christian retreat a few years ago. We got along so well and had so much in common.

A beloved uncle passed away and left me an inheritance; God rest his soul.

I'm using the money to hold a retreat on a private island off the coast of Massachusetts. It will be a place for good Christian women to gather: no alcohol or drugs, no loud music or dancing. Plenty of quiet time and walks on the beach to reflect and pray.

I would like to invite you to come to Castaway Island for a few weeks this summer as my guest, free of charge. I have taken the liberty of reserving a room for you starting on September 16th. The ferry from Hyannis to Nantucket leaves at noon, and we have a boat from there to the island.

Looking forward to seeing you,
U. Kn…

She hadn't been able to make out the name. The signature was poorly written. No one took any pride in their penmanship anymore.

The retreat was two, maybe three years ago? A few nice, respectable women had attended. What was that woman's name, the one she always sat next to at dinner? Ursula something? Knott? Nottingham? Something like that. Yes, it must be that woman.

She thought about the newspaper articles about the private island in the last couple of years. A Hollywood starlet had recently owned it for a short time. If she remembered correctly, a millionaire bought it from the actress slut.

Now, God was going to clean it up and make it the home of a Christian retreat. *And I'm being rewarded with a free vacation!* She could not have afforded such a wonderful trip. Her pension barely covered her rent and bills. With the economy in the trash, the dividends from her investments had been few and far between during the last year. Too bad she couldn't remember who this Mrs. Knott was—or was it Miss?

Thirty-year-old Virginia Campbell removed her red-framed glasses, closed her eyes, and leaned back against the ferry's orange plastic headrest. She pulled her brown corduroy coat tighter around herself, wishing she could afford a new one. Oh well. "Beggars can't be choosers," her grandfather always said. Thank the goddess, this opportunity miraculously appeared. Her savings were almost gone, and she couldn't secure a teaching assignment anywhere.

A cloud still hung over her head, but it hadn't been her fault. The child's death had been a horrible accident. She'd done everything she could, even risked her own life to save the boy, but the ocean had won. Little Kenny, her charge, had drowned. One minute he was a rambunctious, rebellious five-year-old pushing the limits. In the blink of an eye, a monster wave rose up, knocked them both down, and dragged them back into the ocean. She'd fought with every ounce of strength she had to get to the boy, but she was no match against the power of the sea. Barely clinging to life, she'd been rescued an hour later by the Coast Guard. Kenny's body wasn't recovered until the next day when it washed up on a beach two miles away.

Virgie pulled the letter Mr. Moore had given her from her backpack, put on her red-rimmed glasses, and reread it.

Dear Ms. Campbell,

An acquaintance of mine, Mary Smith, a past employer of yours, recommended you for a position tutoring my children while we are on holiday.

We recently bought Castaway Island off the coast of Massachusetts. We will be there through the New Year and do not want our two sons, ages five and eight, to fall behind in school. Your lodging will be covered, and I have enclosed a check for your first month's salary and a ticket for the noon ferry from Hyannis to Nantucket on Friday, September 16th.

A private boat will meet you and take you to the island.

I hope this is acceptable.

Ms. Una Knowly

She couldn't remember a Mary Smith from any schools where she'd worked, not that she cared. She needed this job, even if it was only temporary. It was a lifesaver. And on Castaway Island, of all places. Virgie was a big fan of the actress Grace Taylor, who had owned the island for a short time, having bought it as a wedding present for her new husband, Buck Something or Other. How exciting would it be to visit the island, to walk through the same halls and rooms Grace had? It was just too crazy to imagine. How did she get so lucky?

At thirty-five, Phyllis Long, Phyl to her friends, was no slouch. Her short brown hair and steel-blue eyes caught the attention of many women, gay and straight. Men, too, for that matter, but Phyl couldn't have cared less what the men thought.

Phyl eyed the woman across from her. She was attractive, and the red glasses were kind of sexy, in a naughty teacher kind of way. And there was something mysterious about her, but Phyl couldn't put her finger on it. She shook her head. This was no time to be thinking about her love life. She needed to concentrate on the job.

The ugly little man with a mop of black hair, bushy eyebrows, and a thin mustache had shown up out of the blue at her office and introduced himself as Mr. Moore. He'd handed her a contract to ghostwrite a book about Castaway Island for a woman named Knolles, a check for five thousand dollars, and the promise of ten thousand once the book was done. Phyl had pressed him for more details, but other than the requirement that no one was to know she was writing the book, the little rodent of a man refused to say anything more.

"That's all the details I can give you, Ms. Long. Take it or leave it," he said. "Ms. Knolles is a private person and likes to keep things close to her chest, if you know what I mean."

Phyl could only imagine what the reclusive Ms. Knolles's chest looked like. She shook her head; for all she knew, the Knolles woman could be eighty.

Moore handed her a ticket for the noon ferry leaving on September 16th, from Barnstable to Nantucket. "A private boat will be waiting for you at the dock in Nantucket and deliver you to Castaway Island." He replaced a snug black bowler on his head.

Who wears a hat like that in this century?

"Questions?" Moore asked.

Phyl scrunched her eyebrows together and met his gaze. "Would you answer them if I did?"

"Probably not," the man said as he tipped his hat and shuffled out the door.

It was the strangest book deal she'd ever made. *But why not?* Spending time on a beautiful island might do her some good. She could work on her tan, breathe some fresh air, and get back to running. God knew she'd slacked off her workout routine while writing the last book. This might be just what she needed.

On the noon ferry to Nantucket, Willie Kerrel opened her journal and reviewed the list of guests she'd be keeping an eye on in her role as private security: *Tamara Miller, Catherine Ames, Darcy McDonald, Dr. Emery Brennan, Judge Joan Hathorne, Virginia Campbell, Phyllis Long, and the servants—a married couple named Theo and Rosie Roberts.*

She closed the notebook and drummed her fingers on it. As she leaned back, she adjusted the short-barrel revolver holstered on her hip and closed her eyes. *This should be easy enough.*

Seated on the ferry, recently retired Judge Joan Hathorne, her chin tipped up slightly like she was looking down on the world from on high, read *The New York Times*'s morning edition. She looked up with a sneer and cursed the snowflakes who banned smoking on the ferry. Going several hours without nicotine made her usual coarse personality even more contentious.

She glanced at the elderly man across from her. He needed a bath and a change of clothes. She wondered if he was homeless, wasting his days going back and forth across the ocean on the ferry. He appeared to be either asleep or passed out. It was hard to tell. Joan studied him. *There should be places for degenerates like him. Workhouses, like in the old days. Put 'em to work.*

She returned her focus to the political section of the paper and smiled. If everything went as planned, soon, her name would be in the headlines. She planned to announce her run for Congress, depending on how this trip went. It was a natural next step in her career. She'd made quite a name for herself as the "hanging judge," tough on crime and tougher on those unfortunate enough to appear in her courtroom.

At first, she wasn't sure politics would be the right fit. She didn't like the way people played games in Washington. She thought of herself as someone who shot straight from the hip. She wouldn't make backroom deals. But Mr. Moore, an assistant to Mrs. Knolles, pointed out how that was precisely what she did with prosecutors and lowly defense attorneys whenever she called them into her chambers, twisting their arms until they agreed to a plea deal. She looked down her nose from high upon her throne, stared menacingly at the accused, and convinced them it was in their best interest to take the deal or risk years in one of Massachusetts' prisons. Rarely did anyone insist on going to trial. Rarer still were the few who beat the rap.

Joan ran a hand through her steel-gray hair and looked at her blue, Swiss-made Portofino watch. It was still an hour from Nantucket before catching a private boat to the island. She rifled through her leather bag and pulled out the perfectly penned letter Mr. Moore had given her from Mrs. Knolles. Moore had described Mrs. Knolles as a "kingmaker," bankrolling politicians who shared her conservative ideals.

Dearest Joan,

I've followed your career for several years and appreciate your strong stance on crime and punishment. I believe you would make a fine congresswoman.

God knows Massachusetts needs a woman like you in Washington to save us from those liberal idiots.

I would like to discuss putting together a campaign for the next election. Please join me for a few days at my home on Castaway Island, Friday, September 16–19. Take the noon ferry from Barnstable to Nantucket. A private boat will be waiting on the Washington dock to take you to the island.

I look forward to working with you to make Massachusetts something to be proud of again.

It was signed with a flourish, *Mrs. U.N. Knolles.*

She shoved the letter back into her bag, crossed her arms, and thought about where she was headed. Castaway Island had been in the news often over the last few years. Rumors swirled around its ownership. Bought and sold several times recently, it also had a history of unfortunate events. One owner's wife died in a boating accident. A year later, a guest of the new owner drowned in a seemingly calm area off the beach. Last year, gossip rags reported that Hollywood star Grace Taylor had bought the island for her new husband as a wedding present. But they divorced six months later, and it went back up for sale. She hadn't heard much about the new owner, U.N. Knolles, and

Mr. Moore hadn't been much help. He was tight-lipped, only saying everything would be explained at their meeting. Joan uncrossed her arms and leaned back. A feeling of foreboding encompassed her. She didn't like mysteries.

Thirty minutes later, the ferry bumped against the dock several times as it pulled into Nantucket. The old man across from Joan sat up and stared at her. "The sea is as fickle as a woman!"

Joan ignored him.

The old man belched loudly. "There's a squall coming."

"No, no, it's a beautiful day," Joan said as she stood.

"There's a storm ahead. I can feel it in my bones," the man said with a snarl.

"Perhaps you're right." She didn't want to waste time arguing with him.

The old man stood and teetered back and forth with the sway of the ship. Joan followed him to the exit. Before the man stepped onto the gangplank, he turned around and looked at Joan. "Watch and pray…Watch and pray. Judgment day is at hand." He fell backward on the walkway and lay spread eagle for a few seconds before pushing himself into a sitting position. "The day of judgment is close. You should take heed." He stood, squared his shoulders, and limped away.

Joan stood in place, appalled. "What the hell was that?" she said aloud before a gentle push from behind got her moving again.

CHAPTER TWO

Friday, Early afternoon

An unassuming young man stood at the end of the dock holding a sign that read: CASTAWAY ISLAND. Once the seven women had gathered around him, he told them his name was Adam. He then explained that the private boat could only carry six people and their luggage, so it would need to make two trips. The boat would return in an hour and a half to pick up Dr. Brennan, who was on the afternoon ferry. Adam tucked the sign under his arm. "Would someone volunteer to wait and ride out with the doctor?"

Virgie raised her hand. "I'll wait."

Adam smiled at her. "Thank you."

Phyl stood across from Virgie and smiled at the realization that she was the woman with the red glasses from the ferry. She was even more attractive without the glasses. She smiled at her. "I'll wait with you if that's all right. It'll be less crowded on the next boat."

Virgie's eyes scanned Phyl from head to toe. "Sure."

"Okay, everyone else, please follow me. I'll show you to the boat." He picked up Catherine's suitcase and headed toward a gate marked *Members Only.*

"Thank you for volunteering." Catherine nodded to Virgie before following the young man down the pier.

Phyl held out her hand. "I'm Phyllis Long. My friends call me Phyl."

"Virginia Campbell, but I go by Virgie." She grasped the outstretched hand.

Phyl bent over and picked up her suitcase. "How about we get something to drink while we wait?" She pointed to the café across the street from the ferry parking lot.

"Perfect. It might be my last chance to have a cocktail for a while." Virgie picked up her bag and hitched her backpack on her shoulder.

"Why's that?" Phyl asked as they waited for a couple on a moped to ride by.

Virgie stepped off the curb and said, "I'm here to work. I've been hired to tutor the Knowlys' children."

Phyl stopped halfway across the street and looked at Virgie. *Did she say Knowly?* "Ms. Knolles has children? I pictured her as an eighty-year-old spinster."

Virgie, who had walked a few steps ahead of Phyl, pointed to the oncoming group of Segway riders and motioned to the other side of the street. Once safely on the other side, she said, "The letter said two boys ages five and seven."

Phyl laughed as they took a seat at an empty table. "I guess she can't be eighty years old then, can she?"

"No, I doubt Mrs. Knowly's anywhere close to eighty."

Phyl scrunched her eyebrows together and cocked her head to the side. "Knowly? Isn't it, Knolles?"

Virgie shook her head. "No, my letter was signed, Mrs. Knowly."

A server who looked like he'd spent too much time sunning himself on the beach appeared. Both Phyl and Virgie ordered Cape Cods.

"Have you been to Nantucket before?" Phyl asked.

Virgie shook her head. "No, but it looks like a nice place to spend some time. Have you?"

"Yes. A few years ago, I was invited to spend the summer with a...a friend." Phyl thought better of telling Virgie that she'd spent a summer on Nantucket interviewing a famous rock star for a book she'd been commissioned to ghostwrite.

"Must be nice to have friends like that." Virgie smiled up at the server, who had returned with their drinks.

Phyl sipped the cranberry and vodka cocktail and waited for the server to leave before asking, "Have you met Ms. Knolles?"

Virgie shook her head. "No, I received a certified letter from Mrs. Knowly offering me the job. She said a past employer recommended me." She let out a soft chuckle. "I needed a job, and the money was great, so here I am." She took another sip of her drink. "How'd you end up here?"

Not wanting to give away her real purpose, Phyl lied. "A friend of a friend invited me. Said they knew the new owners, the Knolles." She swallowed. "I guess I got the name wrong." But Phyl was sure Mr. Moore had said Knolles, not Knowly.

"There seems to be some confusion."

"Yes, there does," Phyl agreed.

"For instance, I didn't know guests would be on the island. The letter made it sound like it was their private home. But now it sounds like we're going to a hotel or B&B."

Phyl nodded. She'd thought the same thing but didn't voice it since she was pretending to be a guest. "It does seem strange that she didn't mention that to you."

"I guess it doesn't matter either way."

"Probably not. I hope you'll have some free time to relax and explore the island when you're not with the kids. Maybe we could go for a walk on the beach?"

Virgie froze, her eyes widening. She took a deep breath and slowly let it out, relaxing her shoulders. "I'm not much for the ocean or beach."

"But you took a job on an island. In the middle of an ocean."

Virgie half-smiled. "I know it doesn't make a lot of sense."

Phyl narrowed her eyes but smiled. "I get the feeling there's more to the story."

Virgie looked off into the distance. "I'd rather not talk about it. At least not today."

"Okay, but I'm a good listener if you ever need to talk to someone."

"Thanks, I'll keep it in mind." Virgie changed the subject. "Tell me about you. You don't have a Boston accent. Where are you from?"

"California. I grew up in the Bay Area. My parents and sister still live in the same house I grew up in."

"How'd you end up on the East Coast?"

The sun had risen higher in the sky, and the temperature along with it. Phyl pulled her sweatshirt over her head. The sleeveless blue T-shirt she wore put her well-toned arms on display. Virgie's eyebrows lifted in appreciation.

Phyl sat up straighter. "I played soccer in high school. I was offered a scholarship to Boston University, so I took it, thinking I'd return home after graduating. But I met a girl and ended up staying."

Virgie raised an eyebrow. "And the girl?"

Phyl laughed. "It only lasted a year. But I was in a graduate program by then and had made a life here, so I stayed." She drained the last of her cocktail. "What about you?"

"Not so fast. I still have questions." She finished her drink. "Soccer player, huh?"

Phyl nodded and grinned.

"Still play?"

Before answering, Phyl pointed to their empty glasses and raised an eyebrow.

"Sure."

Phyl motioned the server over and ordered another round of Cape Cods. "I still play in a recreation league in Provincetown during the summer."

"What about the rest of the year?"

"I do some long-distance biking and yoga. What about you?"

"I ride a bike, but not long distance. I love to hike, though, weather allowing."

The server returned with their drinks, set them in the middle of the table, and retreated.

Phyl picked up her drink and took a sip. "You don't have an East Coast accent either, more Midwestern. How'd you end up here?"

Virgie gazed at the ferry pulling away from the dock for its return trip to the mainland. She turned back to Phyl with a smile that didn't quite reach her eyes. "I was born in Portland, Oregon, not Maine. My father was a cop. He was killed when my mother was pregnant. When I was five, my mother was killed in a car accident. My grandparents raised me in Kansas."

Phyl reached out and covered Virgie's hand with her own. "I'm so sorry."

Virgie gave her a smile that looked forced. "I moved out when I was eighteen. I wanted to go to college, but my grandparents refused to help me. My grandfather was a pastor at an ultraconservative church. He didn't believe women needed a college education to be wives and mothers."

Phyl leaned back in her chair. "Seriously? There are still people who think like that?"

"I don't know about everywhere else, but in rural Kansas, yes, there are people who still think like that." Virgie picked up her drink and took a sip. "I worked my way through Kansas State, figured out I was gay, and realized Kansas was not going to be a safe place for me. I moved to California, met a woman, fell in love, and moved with her to Massachusetts. She broke my heart a year later." Virgie exhaled. "End of story."

Phyl grinned. "I doubt that. I think there's a lot more to Virginia Campbell." She winked and raised her glass. "I look forward to finding out."

Virgie raised her glass, but her eyes were dull as their glasses clinked together.

Adam escorted the other guests to the private marina at the far end of the dock. As they followed the young man, Joan marveled at the gigantic yachts and meticulously maintained sailboats as they continued down the walkway. The wealth on display, just in the marina alone, was mind-boggling.

"How much do you think something like that costs?" Willie asked Joan, who walked beside her.

Joan turned her head slightly and looked at Willie. "Don't I know you?" She hoped the woman wasn't someone who had been a defendant in her courtroom.

"Sort of," Willie said as they continued down the walkway. "I used to be a cop. My name's Willie Kerrel. I testified in your courtroom a few times." Willie held out her hand to the judge.

Joan didn't take the offered hand. "Yes, I remember now." She looked straight ahead and continued walking.

When the group reached the end of the dock, they found an attractive woman with sun-streaked blond hair leaning against a shiny pontoon boat that looked like it had just come off the showroom floor. The woman was one of those people whose age was hard to determine, neither young nor old. She was wearing a tank top and cargo shorts, and in place of her left leg was a titanium prosthesis. Her face was weather-beaten from years spent outdoors, but her blue eyes sparkled, and her smile was infectious. A cardboard box sat on the ground next to her feet.

She pushed away from the boat and strolled over. "Welcome, ladies. My name's Frankie Nugent." She looked at Catherine. "And you are?"

"Catherine Ames."

Frankie nodded. "Welcome aboard, Catherine." Turning to Tamara, she smiled. "And you are?"

Tamara batted her eyelashes and flashed a brilliant smile. "I'm Tamara Miller. I'm pleased to meet you."

Frankie chuckled. "Happy to meet you too." She looked at Joan Hathorne. "And you, ma'am?"

Joan stood up straight and pulled back her shoulders. "Joan Hathorne." She had the low, gravelly voice of someone who had smoked a pack a day for many years.

"Nice to meet you, Joan." Frankie turned to Willie. "And you are?"

Willie held out her hand. "Willie Kerrel."

Frankie shook the outstretched hand. "Welcome, Willie." She looked over Joan's shoulder at Darcy and smiled. "And last but not least?"

Darcy reluctantly stepped forward. "Darcy McDonald."

"Welcome, Darcy." Frankie rubbed her hands together and smiled at the group. "Is everyone ready to head to the island? The boat's ready to go."

Catherine looked at the boat skeptically. "It looks more suited for pulling a skier on a lake. Are you sure it's ocean-worthy?"

Frankie smiled. "She's a fine boat, plenty big enough for the crossing. It can hold fourteen people. But with all the luggage, I thought it would be more comfortable with only six or seven at a time."

"Well, it's a beautiful day," Tamara chimed in, her blond hair shimmering in the sun. "I can't wait to get to the island."

"It's a wonderful day to be on the water," Frankie said as she picked up the cardboard box and placed it on the driver's seat. Turning back, she offered to help Catherine in the boat.

Catherine took Frankie's hand reluctantly and stepped aboard. The others, handing their luggage over the side, climbed aboard one at a time.

"Please make yourselves comfortable. Help yourselves to wine and beer. It's in the cooler under the rear seat, and snacks are under the seat next to that." Frankie grinned as she secured the cardboard box under the steering wheel.

In a huff, Catherine sat down in the rear of the boat and crossed her arms. "I don't consume alcohol."

Frankie smiled at her. "Water and nonalcoholic beverages are in the blue ice chest."

Thirty minutes later, they could no longer see Nantucket. Two miles to the east, the faint outline of Castaway Island rose above the horizon.

Tamara took a sip from her plastic champagne flute as she snapped pictures with her cell phone. "I thought it would be different. It's not what I imagined," she said to Darcy, who'd been quiet since they'd arrived in Nantucket.

Darcy looked down at the shorter woman. "What were you expecting?" she asked as she took a swallow from a bottle of German beer.

Tamara shoved her phone into the back pocket of her indigo-blue skinny jeans. "I thought it would be closer to Nantucket, and we'd be able to see a big white house with lots of windows." No house of any size or color could be seen from that far away, only the dark gray outline of a flat rock sticking out of the blue-green water. Tamara felt a chill run up her spine and pulled her leather coat tighter around her as she went to refill her glass. No, it was nothing like she'd imagined.

Frankie stood behind the wheel of the brand new, twenty-five-foot Avalon Catalina Platinum Pontoon boat. After maneuvering out of the marina and into the open sea, she discreetly glanced at each passenger. It was an odd assortment—nothing like what she'd experienced with the previous owners. Celebrities had arrived and departed at all hours of the day and night during the six months Grace Taylor and her husband had owned the island. The parties had been legendary. When Robert Masterson owned it, his ultra-wealthy visitors drank only the most expensive wines and whiskeys. Most of his guests had flown into Nantucket on private planes, avoiding the lower classes on the ferries.

This group didn't seem to have anything in common. They didn't even seem to know each other. It was strange. In fact, everything about the Knowleses was strange. As far as Frankie knew, the Knowleses hadn't been out to the island since they'd purchased it. Frankie certainly hadn't met them; she'd only had dealings with the obnoxious Mr. Moore. But she wasn't going to complain since she was well paid, and it was easy work.

She snuck a peek at each of the guests. Catherine, the old spinster who didn't drink alcohol wouldn't be much fun sitting around the fire on a cold night. The stern, no-nonsense-looking woman, Joan, with her back as straight as a board and probably a stick up her ass as well, didn't look like a partier. The redhead, Willie, was a beauty for a woman her age. Frankie wondered what the story was with the other middle-aged woman, Darcy. She'd be attractive if she ever smiled. The youngest one, Tamara, was precisely what she'd expected. She had money, as shown by the leather coat and those shoes with red soles. What were those called? Jimmy Something or Other? And she had gone directly for the authentic French champagne, no domestic beer or wine for her. Yes, she was the party girl in the group.

It was an odd assortment of guests. *Well, at least this group won't cause any damage to the place, and the Robertses, the hired help, won't have a big mess to clean up after they've all left.* Frankie stretched her neck from side to side and lifted her face to the sun as she expertly maneuvered the boat over the white-capped water.

With a full flute of champagne, Tamara made her way to the center of the boat and stood next to Frankie. She smiled flirtatiously. "How did the island get its name?" she asked, taking a sip from the flute.

Frankie took in the sexy, younger woman and smiled. "It goes back to the American Revolution. Supposedly in the last year of the war, a British ship set sail for England with a hundred prisoners of war and got caught in a hurricane. It sank somewhere between Nantucket and the island. The remains of the ship have never been recovered."

"I'm surprised. I thought hunting for sunken ships was a thing."

"It is, but the tides out here move things around. It could be underneath us right now and drift away tomorrow."

"Did anyone survive?"

Frankie nodded. "Some of the soldiers and prisoners washed up on the island. They were stranded for almost a year. Somehow, they managed to work together and not kill each other. Shortly after the war ended, a merchant ship heading to South America spotted smoke on the island and investigated. Only fifty men were still alive, half British, half American."

"It's named Castaway Island in their honor?"

Frankie nodded again. "It's always been a privately owned island, so someone could rename it. No one ever has."

Tamara continued to stand next to Frankie, watching a flock of seagulls fly overhead.

"What brings you out to the island?" Frankie asked.

"I'm meeting some sorority sisters from U of A. I haven't seen them since we graduated."

"U of A?"

"University of Alabama." Tamara smiled. "My parents are alumni. It wouldn't have been my first choice, but it's a family tradition. And Daddy wouldn't pay for anywhere else." She shrugged. "So, it was U of A or nothing." She took another sip of champagne and asked, "Where did you go to school?"

Frankie laughed out loud. "I didn't go to college. After I graduated high school in 2004, I joined the Navy."

"That makes you…thirty-four or five?"

"Thirty-five," Frankie said. "It was a few years after 9/11. I came from a military family, so enlisting was only natural."

"Is that how you—" Tamara stopped herself. "Sorry, sometimes I forget my boundaries."

"No, it's fine." Frankie gave her a weak smile. "Yes, that's when I lost my leg. I was on a Navy supply plane over Afghanistan. We were dropping boxes of food to a remote village. Al-Qaeda rebels shot us down. I was the only one who survived." Frankie stared straight ahead, her face an emotionless mask.

Tamara put her hand on Frankie's shoulder. "Oh, my God. I'm so sorry."

"Thanks, but it's been ten years. I'm doing okay."

"How did you end up here?"

"After I was rescued, the Navy sent me to Germany. I was in the hospital for six months. Then at Walter Reed Medical Center in Maryland for another six months of rehab. When I was released, I wanted to go where it was quiet and peaceful. So, I came home to Nantucket."

"Sounds like a wonderful place. Maybe I'll check it out when I return from my reunion with the girls." She gave Frankie another flirtatious smile.

"If you do, I'd be happy to show you around. We have some of the best beaches in the world."

"Lucky for me, I brought a bikini." Tamara winked.

As the boat cut through the gentle waves, the island grew larger. Tamara jumped to the front of the boat and started taking pictures. *This is more what I had in mind.* From the west side, which faced Nantucket, they could only see trees and a small beach protected by solid, menacing cliffs. The cliffs continued to protect the island as they rounded the south side. The view of the white, three-story Victorian house that faced south was spectacular.

Frankie expertly maneuvered the boat into the tiny natural inlet that provided a safe, secluded harbor from the rough ocean currents. She shut the engine off and glided up alongside what looked to be a recently built dock, big enough for only one boat.

"I'll bet it's not easy to land this thing in bad weather," Tamara shouted over the roar of the waves crashing against the cliffs.

"Can't land on Castaway Island when a nor'easter's blowin'," Frankie yelled. "Sometimes the island's cut off for days, even a week at a time."

Frankie jumped onto the dock and tied the front and rear of the boat securely to the large metal cleats attached to the pier. "Leave your bags here. I'll bring them to the house before I return for the others." She held out her hand to help Catherine out of the boat. "Just go up the stairs to the house." She pointed to the forty or so stairs carved into the side of the cliff and a handrail that looked new. "The Knowleses haven't arrived yet, but the staff will make you comfortable in the meantime."

"Thank you, Frankie." Tamara winked as she discreetly handed Frankie a fifty-dollar bill.

Frankie smiled. "My pleasure."

Darcy was the first one up the stairs. She prided herself on staying in shape and not letting herself go after she turned fifty-five. It would have been easy enough; God knew she had every reason to. Her daily routine began with a five-mile run—not a jog, a run—then an hour of weights in her home gym. Three times a week she attended a yoga class to stay limber. Her hair might be turning gray, but she wouldn't let turning fifty-five slow her down or be an excuse to wallow in depression.

As she stepped onto the front lawn, the view of the Atlantic Ocean and the sun sparkling off the water like diamonds took her breath away. The grounds were picture-perfect. A grove of swamp maple trees peeked out from behind the house, and two ancient weeping willows stood on either end. The symmetrical two-story Cape Cod house was impressive. The craftsmanship and attention to detail were superb. The structure was painted a creamy white. Its steeply sloping roof, black exterior shutters, and bright red door exuded a traditional New England charm. On the first floor, two large casement windows flanked either side of the front door, and five matching windows were spaced evenly across the second. Two dormers rose out of the roof like soldiers standing guard.

But something made her uneasy. It was too quiet. Aside from the ocean's roar and a flock of seagulls passing overhead, she heard no other sounds. Where were the other guests? She thought Tammy and Tiger would already be here. Strangely, the woman on the boat hadn't mentioned anything about other guests besides a doctor and the two who volunteered to wait for the next boat. Before she could worry more about it, the others stepped onto the lawn. Tamara held up her phone, talking and shooting a video. Catherine brought up the rear.

"Oh my." Catherine bent over to catch her breath.

Darcy put a hand on the older woman's back. "Are you all right?"

Catherine at once straightened and stepped away. "Yes, of course I am." Her face, however, was as red as a raspberry and her breathing heavy.

From the house doorway, a figure appeared. Sporting short brown hair, a slight but muscular build, and dressed in crisp black slacks and a starched, tailored white shirt, it wasn't easy to tell whether the person was male or female. Darcy smiled to herself. She'd always been attracted to the androgynous type. What did they call it now? Gender fluid? Nonbinary? She'd have to Google it so she didn't misuse the term and offend anyone.

"Welcome, everyone. Please come in," they said.

The voice sounded more feminine than masculine, and Darcy hummed her approval. She preferred sex with a woman, but on the few occasions she and her husband had had sex, it was pleasant enough. Darcy smiled at the thought of getting to know this handsome young person. *Things just got a lot more interesting.*

Two hours, three Cape Cods, two lobster rolls, and an order of crab cakes later, Virgie and Phyl heard the low rumble of the incoming ferry. "I guess we should head back," Phyl said, motioning to the server for their bill.

Virgie reached into her backpack and pulled out her wallet. "Let me get it."

Phyl shook her head. "No, no. I'll get it. I'm the one who insisted on lobster rolls and crab cakes. You can get it next time."

Virgie raised an eyebrow. "Next time?"

"Maybe when we get back?"

Virgie smiled. "Maybe."

They grabbed their bags and slowly returned to where they'd met Adam, who'd earlier been holding the sign for Castaway Island. The sun had moved to the western sky, and the breeze off the water had picked up, but the temperature was still in the midseventies.

"It's been a perfect day," Virgie said as she shifted her backpack from one shoulder to the other.

Phyl laughed. "All I did was invite myself to wait with you."

"Why didn't you go with the others?" Virgie asked as she tucked a lock of hair behind her ear.

Phyl took a deep breath and let it out. "The truth?"

Virgie hesitated, then nodded.

"I saw you on the ferry. You had on red-rimmed glasses."

Virgie scrunched her eyebrows together, not understanding what Phyl was getting at. "Okay?"

Phyl's face reddened slightly. "I thought the glasses were kinda sexy."

Virgie let out a laugh. "Really? My glasses?"

Phyl shrugged. "What can I say? Not too many people can pull off red glasses."

Virgie smiled. "I guess that's a compliment?"

"Oh yeah. It's a compliment." Phyl grinned.

While they waited, they talked and watched passengers disembark from the ferry.

"Good afternoon, Ms. Long and Ms. Campbell." Adam had quietly walked up behind them. "Thank you for volunteering to wait. I hope it wasn't too much of an inconvenience."

Both women smiled and shook their heads. "No inconvenience at all," Phyl said as she winked at Virgie.

"Good. I believe that's Dr. Brennan walking up the hill now."

Virgie and Phyl turned toward an attractive woman Virgie guessed to be about forty, walking up the slight incline. Wearing black slacks and a white tailored dress shirt, she looked like she was there to work, not relax. When the woman grew closer, Adam asked, "Dr. Brennan?"

"Yes." Emery smiled.

"Great," he said, "my name is Adam, and this is Ms. Long and Ms. Campbell." He motioned to each woman.

Phyl held out her hand. "I'm Phyl," she said.

Emery shook Phyl's outstretched hand. "Emery. It's nice to meet you."

Virgie offered her hand to the doctor. "I'm Virgie."

"Emery," she said with a smile. "I didn't know there were others going to the island."

Virgie and Phyl both raised their shoulders slightly. "Neither did we," Virgie said.

All three looked at Adam for an explanation. His eyes grew to the size of quarters, and he took a step back. "I don't know anything about the guest list. I was only hired a week ago to escort everyone to the boat." He took another step back. "It's this way." He pointed to a gate that led to a private marina. "Please follow me."

Before entering the house, Tamara paused to post the video on her Instagram but couldn't get cell service. *That's not good.*

Stepping over the threshold into the house, she was delighted to see the rows of shiny liquor bottles. *Interesting that the front room of the house is designed like an Irish pub*, she mused. *A high-class pub at that.*

A redwood bar ran the length of the far wall. Behind it, bottles of various colors and shapes were on display—blue, black, brown, transparent, round, square, and even triangular. Some were costly upper-end labels and extremely rare. The ones she didn't recognize she looked forward to sampling. A tall wine refrigerator stood in the corner of the room, but the tinted glass door made it difficult to see what treasures it held. An ice bucket with an open magnum of Dom Perignon sat on the bar. "Now you're talking," Tamara said as she made her way to it.

The androgynous-looking person walked up to the group and cleared their throat. "Welcome, ladies. My name is Theo Roberts, and this is my wife, Rosie."

Tamara noticed Darcy frown at the news and wondered why. Tamara on the other hand, smiled at the woman's spiky, platinum-blond hair that reminded her of a petite version of P!nk. That thought made her wonder if P!nk had ever partied at the house when Grace Taylor owned it. However, the diminutive woman before her was not self-assured and boisterous like the rock star. She looked reserved and nervous, eyes darting from person to person.

Theo continued, "Unfortunately, while you were in transit, we received word from Ms. Knowles that she will be delayed until tomorrow. It's a business issue," they said. "Ms. Knowles sent her apologies and asked that you make yourselves at home.

My wife and I will make sure you have everything you need. If there's anything we can do to make your stay more pleasant, don't hesitate to ask."

"Where are the other guests?" Tamara asked.

Theo smiled. "Ms. Nugent will return with our three other guests in time for dinner, which will be served at six o'clock."

Tamara scrunched her eyebrows together. "No, not them. I'm meeting some of my sorority sisters." She looked around the room at the others.

"And I'm meeting several colleagues for a reunion," Darcy said.

Catherine said from her chair at one of the small round tables, "I'm here to attend a Christian retreat." She looked around the room. "This does not look very Christian to me," she huffed.

Tamara looked from one servant to the other. Theo looked confused. Rosie's eyes grew wide, and she chewed on her lower lip.

Joan pushed herself away from the wall. "Theo, what the hell is going on here?"

Tamara saw the deer in the headlights look that crossed Theo's face. It was quickly replaced with a mask of someone trying to appear in control.

Theo stood up straight and pushed their shoulders back. "You're Judge Hathorne, aren't you?"

Joan nodded. And it's Ms. Hathorne or Joan. I'm no longer on the bench. No need to use the title."

"As you wish," Theo said, then turned to the others. "We don't know of any other guests. We were told to prepare rooms for eight people this week. Perhaps when the Knowleses arrive tomorrow, they'll have the answers."

Joan let out a huff. "This is unacceptable. I'm not going to bother to unpack; if I don't get some answers in the morning, I'll be leaving."

Tamara raised her hand. "Theo, what's the Wi-Fi name and password?"

Theo frowned. "I'm sorry to say there's no Wi-Fi on the island. Sometimes, you can get cell service near the cliff's edge on the west side of the island. But that depends on the weather."

Catherine stood up from her chair and set her hands on her hips. "How do you contact people off the island? What if there's an emergency?"

Theo took a deep breath. They weren't happy with the situation either. "There's a CB radio we use to contact Ms. Nugent and the Coast Guard if there's an emergency," they said with a frown. "But again, it's not always reliable in a storm."

"Well, shit." Tamara narrowed her eyes. "My Insta followers will be disappointed. I never go more than an hour or two without updating them."

"Then this may be the perfect time to break your social media habit," Joan said. "It's a waste of time."

Tamara scowled but didn't say anything. When Joan turned away, Tamara raised her middle finger and silently mouthed, "Bitch."

"Ladies, if any of you would like to freshen up, Rosie can show you to your room. Ms. Nugent has brought your bags up, and I will deliver them to the rooms shortly. While we wait for the others, please enjoy refreshments and the lovely day. I understand we are in for a storm tonight."

Two hours later, the boat returned to the island with the three other guests, Virgie, Phyl, and Emery. When they made their way up the stairs to the lawn, it was close to four o'clock, and the summer sun was still high. Virgie stood next to Phyl and admired the view. By the time they'd finished their third cocktail waiting for the doctor, they'd formed a friendship of sorts. Phyl had come clean and explained that she wasn't visiting the island to meet a friend. She confided in Virgie that she had been contracted to ghostwrite a book about the island. That was her real reason for being invited. Virgie had agreed to keep her secret since she was also in Knowly's employ. As far as anybody else knew, Phyl was on vacation.

Emery walked up next to them and watched a seagull sail slowly overhead. This was just what she needed, even if it was only for a few days. Too bad it couldn't be longer, but her business partner, Dr. Nichols, was young and inexperienced. He was an excellent doctor but not ready to run the business. Someday soon she hoped to walk away and enjoy life. God knew life was short, and the slightest misstep could end it all.

"Interesting choice of trees," Emery said.

Phyl and Virgie turned to look at her. "How so?" Phyl asked.

Emery pointed to the half dozen Italian cypress trees that lined the terrace. "The cypress certainly isn't native to the area. I wonder if they know that they represent death and mourning?" She pointed to the weeping willow trees. "In some cultures, weeping willows in front of a house shows that the family has had an unhappy life. Some say you should never buy a house with a weeping willow in the garden since the unhappiness could still be present."

"How do you know all that?" Virgie asked.

"I'm an amateur botanist," she said. "I'm going to head up to the house. It's been a long day. I'm beat." She turned and headed toward the big white house.

Smiling to herself, Emery stepped onto the terrace and found an older woman sitting on a lounger reading a book, a cigarette dangling from between her lips. She looked familiar. Where had she seen this older woman with graying hair and steel-blue eyes? Then it hit her: Judge Joan Hathorne. Emery had testified in her courtroom as an expert witness several times over the years. The judge had always looked at expert witnesses with a skeptical hawklike focus. She was intimidating as hell and held great sway with a jury. She knew just how to manipulate them into a conviction. Behind her back, everyone called her "the hanging judge," since an accused defendant seldom stood a chance in her court.

Strange place to run into her.

Joan Hathorne laid her book on her lap and watched the familiar-looking woman approach. *Is that Dr. Brennan? Why in hell is she here?* Thinking back to the times the doctor had testified in her courtroom left a bad taste in her mouth. Doctors who claimed to be "experts" and claimed that "women's issues" could cause a woman to commit a crime were charlatans as far as Joan was concerned. People who committed criminal acts had a weak constitution. It had nothing to do with menstruation or postpartum depression—pure bullshit. But the doctor was persuasive on the witness stand, and juries loved her smile and confidence. Her good looks didn't hurt either.

Emery smiled as she approached. "Hello, Your Honor."

Joan removed the cigarette from her mouth. "I'm no longer a judge. No need to use that title." She continued to look out to sea, refusing to look at Emery.

"All right."

"Refreshments are inside, and dinner is at six."

"Okay. Are our hosts inside?"

"They're not here."

"What? Why not?"

"Delayed for some reason. On top of that, there's no Wi-Fi, and you have to traipse to the other side of the island to find cell service." Joan finally looked up at Emery. "Something's not right about this place. Not right at all."

Emery furrowed her brow, not sure what to say.

Joan looked toward the water. "Has Frankie left?"

"I'm not sure."

Joan continued to stare off at the horizon, then asked, "Are you meeting people here?"

Not wanting to violate the confidentiality clause of her contract, Emery shook her head. "No, just a few days of rest."

Joan didn't say a word and turned back to her book. Emery shrugged, feeling like she'd been dismissed, and continued into the house.

It had been a long day, and Virgie longed for a nap before dinner. She found Rosie in the kitchen. "Excuse me, would you mind showing me where my room is?"

Rosie nodded and, without a word, turned and walked to the staircase. At the top of the first staircase were two hallways, one to the east and one to the west. Another staircase led to the third floor. Rosie turned east and walked to the last door at the end of the hall.

"This is your room." She placed a key in the lock and opened the door.

Virgie peeked inside; it was delightful. Two floor-to-ceiling windows looked out over the front lawn, flooding the room with light. The windows were open, allowing in the sea breeze. Two wingback chairs faced the windows. A beautiful patchwork quilt covered a queen-size, four-poster bed. Matching nightstands on either side held antique lamps. Her suitcase rested on a stand at the foot of the bed. On the opposite wall was a small desk with another antique lamp and a wooden chair. On the same wall, a door stood open, revealing a white- and rose-tiled bathroom.

"I hope it is to your liking, Ms. Campbell," Rosie said without looking at her.

"It's lovely. Are you sure this is my room?" Virgie asked.

Rosie leaned her head to the side and placed her fists on her hips. "Of course, it is. Why wouldn't it be?"

"Well, these are guest rooms and I'm not a guest."

Rosie scrunched her eyebrows together. "Of course you're a guest."

Virgie slowly moved her head from side to side. "No, I'm the children's tutor."

"Children? No one said anything about children." Rosie shook her head adamantly. "No arrangements have been made for children."

"Ms. Knowly didn't tell you she had children?" Now it was Virgie who cocked her head to the side and scrunched her eyebrows together. *What the hell is going on here?*

"We haven't met Ms. *Knolles* yet. We only arrived three days ago." Rosie paused. "Mr. Moore hired us. He said he got our names from a previous employer." A strange look crossed her face. "But for the life of us, we don't remember working for the person."

"What other staff do they employ?"

"It's just the two of us. I do the cooking and make up the rooms each day. Theo waits on the guests and does the maintenance. We should be able to manage it. But if there are children…"

"The children will be with me during the day. I don't know about at night. I wasn't hired to be a nanny."

Rosie turned to go. "I guess Ms. Knolles will explain when she gets here tomorrow."

"Rosie, you and Theo keep saying Ms. Knolles. My letter was signed by Ms. Knowly."

"I'm sure Mr. Moore said her name was Knolles." Rosie bit her lower lip and frowned. "A lot of things aren't making sense, are they?"

"No, they aren't. But I suppose we won't get any answers today."

Rosie agreed before slipping out of the room and down the hallway as quietly as a fairy in the mist.

Virgie noticed the windows didn't have screens and wondered briefly about flies and mosquitoes getting into the room, but she let it go. There were too many other things to be concerned with. The delay of Mrs. Knowly—or Knolles—to the island, the staff not knowing anything about the children or the other guests, or who had invited each of them to the island. It was odd. Very odd.

Glancing around the room, Virgie spotted an intricately carved wooden frame on the desk. She picked it up and read a handwritten poem on aged parchment paper.

Ten little castaways went out to dine;
One choked their little self, and then there were Nine.

Nine little castaways stayed up late;
One overslept, and then there were Eight.

Eight little castaways in a procession;
One fell out of line, and then there were Seven.

Seven little castaways chopping up sticks;
One chopped themself in half, and then there were Six.

Six little castaways playing with knives;
One got careless, and then there were Five.

Five little castaways headed for the door;
One fell down, and then there were Four.

Four little castaways went on a spree;
One bumped her head, and then there were Three.

Three little castaways didn't know what to do;
One got an idea, and then there were Two.

Two little castaways sitting in the sun;
One got overheated, and then there was One.

One little castaway playing with a gun;
It went off, and then there were None.

Virgie thought it odd there wasn't a name attributed to the poem. In any case, she thought it morbid. *Why would something like this be in a guest room?* Then it dawned on her. This was Castaway Island. It had been named for the English soldiers and American prisoners of war shipwrecked on the island.

Going to the window, she eased into one of the wingback chairs. She stared out at the sea, taking in the blue-green water and whitecaps on the waves. Although it seemed peaceful today, it was a deception. The beauty of the sea couldn't be trusted. Virgie knew firsthand just how cruel the sea could be, that without warning, it could sneak up and drag a person down into its depths, screams muffled by its watery hand. She would never turn her back on the sea again.

Catherine sat in the wingback chair facing the window and pulled her knitting out of her canvas bag, the sun warming the room.

Theo placed a tray on the table next to her. "Here's your tea, Ms. Ames."

Catherine put down her knitting and looked up at Theo. "Theo, can I ask you a personal question?

Theo took a deep breath. "I suppose so."

"I'm unsure if you're a man or a woman. You look like a young man, but your voice is feminine." Catherine watched Theo stretched their neck from side to side, then roll their shoulders back.

"Neither. I'm gender fluid. Some people refer to it as nonbinary."

Catherine leaned her head to the side slightly. "What does that mean?"

"It means that I don't put a label on my gender." Theo took a slow, deep breath and let it out.

"I don't understand. God made men and women. You're either one or the other."

Theo crossed their arms. "Ms. Ames, I would rather not engage in a discussion about religion with you. Suffice to say, I embrace both the male and female sides of myself. I don't run away from being masculine or feminine. I am both."

Catherine paused to consider what Theo said. "But how do I address you? Is it he or she?"

"I prefer they or them."

Catherine pursed her lips and shook her head as she stared at Theo. "That doesn't make sense."

"I am both male and female, so they and them make perfect sense." Theo smiled slightly. "And until Xe with an 'X' or Ze with a 'Z' catch on, they and them will have to do." Theo straightened their shoulders. "Now, if you'll excuse me, I need to bring in more wood for the fire. It's going to be cold tonight." Theo nodded and left the room.

Catherine looked out the window. They, them, xe, ze, male and female. It was all too confusing. She'd have to pray on it tonight before going to bed.

Tamara relaxed, sinking into the oversized bathtub with a glass of champagne. She closed her eyes, enjoying the scent of lavender that drifted up from the bubbles. She took a deep breath and let it out slowly, relaxing into the luxury. She tried to meditate, forget, and focus on the here and now, not the past. The alcohol helped, but it was only a temporary fix. It wasn't fair. It hadn't been her fault. Why wouldn't her brain let her forget?

After taking a sip from the crystal flute, she rested her head against the back of the tub. She counted slowly, one…two… three…taking a deep breath with each number like her shrink recommended she do to relieve stress. After counting to ten, she gave up and gulped down the rest of the champagne.

Willie stood in front of the full-length mirror and tucked her kelly-green shirt into khaki slacks. Did she look all right? The shirt brought out the green in her eyes. Would anyone notice? No one had been very friendly so far. Other than young Tamara, they all seemed to have a stick up their asses. No matter. She was here to work, not play.

Darcy chewed on her lower lip as she paced the room, thinking about the other guests. What did she know about them, really? Especially Willie…she was too smooth. Darcy was sure she was hiding something.

Phyl walked over to the dresser and grabbed her watch. Seeing the antique frame, she picked it up and read the poem. An interesting touch. It was a little ghoulish, but since it was Castaway Island, it was appropriate in a twisted sort of way. When the bell rang, signaling dinner, she exited her room and noiselessly walked down the hall to the stairs. She smiled when she saw Virgie ahead of her. Maybe the assignment would be more interesting than she'd thought.

Catherine Ames, dressed in black, sat in front of the large window in her room, reading her Bible and whispering to herself, "Isaiah 3:11. 'Woe to the wicked! It will go badly with him, for what he deserves will be done to him.'"

She closed the book and smiled. It was one of her favorite passages. She went to the dresser and picked up a beaded crucifix, pinning it just above her heart. Smiling at herself in the mirror, she knew God protected her for whatever happened this week. After all, she was a pious woman.

CHAPTER THREE

Friday Evening

Darcy was the first one downstairs for dinner. She wanted to talk to Theo without the others around. When Theo entered the dining room with a tray of water glasses, Darcy cleared her throat. "Theo."

Theo stopped and looked up. "Yes, Ms. McDonald, do you need something?"

Darcy shook her head and smiled. "No, no. I was just wondering…I'm not sure how to bring this up, so I'll just jump in. I use the pronouns she and her and wondered what pronouns you preferred."

Theo smiled. "It's kind of you to ask. I prefer they and them."

Darcy returned Theo's smile. "Is it okay if I pass that on to the others?"

Theo let out a small laugh. "I've already had an awkward conversation with Ms. Ames. I don't think she gets it."

"Catherine asked you about pronouns?"

"In a roundabout way," Theo said as they continued to set out the glasses of water.

Darcy put her hands in her pockets and leaned against the wall. "I hope she wasn't rude."

"Not maliciously so," Theo said, brushing a crumb off the table.

"Her religious bias is certainly off-putting."

"Yes, it is, but I'm used to it. I've had to deal with people like her my whole life."

Darcy frowned. "I'm sorry."

Theo shook their head. "No need. It's not your fault." Theo turned their attention back to the water glasses.

"No, but being bisexual, I know how ignorant people can be."

Theo looked up. "Thinking you can't make up your mind? Whether you're gay or straight?"

Darcy nodded. "Exactly. It's tiresome. And disheartening. I've given up on dating. It's not worth the effort."

Joan walked into the room and looked from Darcy to Theo. "What's not worth the effort?"

"Nothing important." Darcy pushed away from the wall. "I need to wash my hands. If you'll excuse me." Darcy smiled as she left.

Joan looked questioningly at Theo. "Did I interrupt something?"

Theo shook their head. "No, just a friendly discussion about pronouns."

Dinner was a pleasant affair. The pork roast was tender, the garlic mashed potatoes creamy, and the asparagus with hollandaise sauce, the perfect vegetable to complement the meal. Theo circled the table pouring coffee, and Rosie served homemade apple pie with vanilla ice cream for dessert. Everyone's spirits had improved and conversation flowed easily.

Having loosened up after three glasses of an excellent Napa Valley cabernet, Joan talked amiably with Emery and Tamara. Catherine chatted with Darcy, and Virgie laughed at something Willie said. Phyl listened in and frowned. Something about Willie rubbed her the wrong way. She looked around the table at the other guests; all seemed to be having a good time. She glanced at the wooden shelf above the buffet table behind Virgie and stood to get a better look at the displayed knickknacks. On closer inspection, she saw ten small figurines carved in wood, all female and all dressed alike. She picked one up and held it out for the group to see. "Aren't these interesting," she said, loud enough to be heard over the conversations.

Virgie turned around in her seat to see. "What is it?"

Phyl handed the figurine to her. "There's ten of them."

Joan wiped her mouth with her napkin before she spoke. "For Castaway Island, I suppose."

Virgie passed the figurine across the table to Willie. "Like the ten little castaways poem in my room."

"Mine too," Willie said.

"And mine," a few others volunteered.

Theo entered the room and added, "Those came with the delivery boat this morning with instructions from Ms. Knowles to display them," they said.

"And the poem in our rooms?" Willie asked, handing the little castaway back to Phyl, who returned it to the shelf.

Theo nodded. "In the same box with the figurines with instructions to place one in each room."

"It's a cute idea," Virgie said.

"Childish, if you ask me." Joan laid her napkin on the table and stood. "Anyone care to join me for an after-dinner drink?"

"A cup of tea would do nicely," Catherine said.

In the front room, the fire roared in the fireplace. Since the large French doors were open, they could hear the waves pounding against the cliffs. Before leaving to make tea, Theo stood behind the bar and poured brandy into several crystal snifters.

Darcy crossed the room and began to close the French doors. "Does anyone mind? Once the sun goes down, it'll get a bit chilly."

Tamara and Catherine sat in front of the fire. "Thank you, Darcy. As much as I like the sound of the ocean, it's too cold to have them open," Catherine said.

Virgie wrapped her arms around her waist. "I hate it."

Everyone turned their attention to her.

Virgie's face reddened a bit. "I don't think this place will be much fun in a storm."

Catherine agreed as she pulled yarn and knitting needles out of her bag, "I can't imagine the place will be open to guests during the winter months," she said. "Getting staff to stay and supplies out here during bad weather would be difficult."

"Impossible at times, I imagine," Phyl agreed.

"I think Mrs. Knott was fortunate to get Theo and Rosie to come here," Catherine said as she began to form a chain with the knitting needles.

Virgie looked at her questioningly. "I'm pretty sure it's Knowly, not Knott," Virgie said as Theo entered the room carrying the cardboard box Frankie had brought from Nantucket and set it down on the coffee table.

"Ms. Knolles's instructions were to open this after dinner," Theo said, then walked away.

"I love surprises." Tamara smiled. "Who's got a knife?"

Phyl stepped up. "I do." She pulled out a small Swiss Army knife and sliced through the tape. She pushed back the flaps and looked inside. There were letter-size, sealed, manila envelopes. She flipped through them. There were nine. On eight were the names of a person in the room. On the ninth was Theo's and Rosie's.

"What's in it?" Tamara bounced on her toes.

Phyl looked up, her forehead wrinkled in uncertainty. "There's nine envelopes. Each one has a name on it."

"Whose names?" Virgie asked.

Phyl looked at her. "Our names."

Joan took charge. "Hand them out. Let's see what's in them."

Phyl removed the envelopes from the box and handed them out one at a time. Virgie and Tamara were the first to open theirs.

Virgie gasped, "Oh my God."

"What the hell is this?" Phyl's eyes narrowed, her face ashen.

The others opened theirs to varying degrees of anger, disbelief, and confusion.

"I don't understand," Catherine said. "Why is someone sending me obituaries of two little girls?"

"That's what's in mine, too," Darcy said.

"Mine too," Emery and Tamara said in unison.

"Theo," Rosie cried out as she ran out of the room to find Theo.

Joan slapped her envelope down on the coffee table. "What the hell is going—"

"Ladies," a deep female voice boomed from behind them, causing everyone to jump. All eyes searched the room, trying to locate where it had come from. The voice continued, "You are charged with the following crimes:

Emery Brennan, Joan Hathorne, Tamara Miller, Darcy McDonald, and Catherine Ames, in 2015, your actions led to the deaths of ten-year-old Alison Rockway and eight-year-old Patrice Timmons.

Phyllis Long, on May first, 2017, you caused the deaths of six schoolchildren.

Virginia Marie Campbell, on August first, 2018, your actions led to the death of five-year-old Kenneth Anthony.

Wilma Anna Kerrel, on April sixteenth, 2019, you caused the death of Timothy Buttons.

Theodora and Rosie Roberts, on December twenty-third, 2019, you caused the death of Madeline Brady.

Do any of the accused have anything to say in their defense?"

CHAPTER FOUR

Friday Night

Outside, the wind crashed against the house, and rain pelted the windows. Inside, the eight women sat stunned, unable to speak. From the doorway, a crash of metal and glass broke the silence. Almost simultaneously, a woman's gasp preceded a loud thud outside the room.

Phyl, closest to the doorway, stepped into the hallway. Theo stood frozen. They'd dropped the serving tray they'd been holding, and porcelain teacups lay on the hardwood floor, shattered into dozens of puzzle pieces. Rosie lay crumpled on the floor a few feet away.

"Doctor, I need your help," Phyl called out.

Emery rushed across the room and knelt next to the young woman. "She's breathing. Help me get her to the sofa."

Phyl and Emery quickly transported her as she was light as a feather.

"Get me a damp towel," Emery said to Theo, who stood nearby in stunned silence.

"Yes, of course. Right away," Theo stammered. Phyl noticed that their hands were shaking.

"Who the hell was that?" Virgie asked, her eyes wide with fear.

"What the hell is going on?" Darcy demanded. "I didn't have anything to do with those girls' deaths."

"Neither did I," Tamara said.

Willie dropped her head into her hands, her shoulders sagged.

Infuriated, Phyl sprang into action. "Where did it come from? Could anyone tell?"

"Who was it? Why would anyone say those things?" Virgie asked, tears streaming down her cheeks.

Phyl looked around the room and along the four walls, looking for clues. Behind the bar, she found a hidden door in the paneling and slid it open. She reached in and flipped the light switch. It was a small windowless room, eight feet wide and twelve feet deep. It appeared to be a recording studio. "I'll be damned. A hidden room."

Virgie, Tamara, Darcy, and Willie rushed over and crowded behind the bar. Inside the small room were several white cabinets. Various types of audio equipment sat on a table, and the backs of two speakers poked out from the wall. Darcy looked at the wall behind the bar where two framed pictures of clowns hung. She removed one picture and found the front of a speaker recessed in the wall.

Phyl looked over the equipment and pushed a button; the same voice rang out, "You are charged with—"

"Stop it! Turn it off," Virgie pleaded.

Phyl pushed the button again and the voice stopped.

Willie's face was red with anger. "Is this a joke? If it is, it's not funny."

"Who in the hell turned it on?" Darcy asked. "There's only one way in or out of the room."

Virgie folded her arms. "It must have been remotely activated. Maybe a Bluetooth device from nearby."

Joan appeared in the doorway. "We need to determine who did this."

"I agree," Willie said, exiting the room, and the others followed.

Theo returned and stood near Catherine, who knelt next to Rosie, praying.

"Excuse me, Ms. Ames," Theo said, placing the wet towel on Rosie's forehead. "Rosie, can you hear me? Are you okay? Come on now, wake up."

Rosie's eyes fluttered open. She looked around the room at each person, visibly afraid.

Emery walked to the sofa. "You'll be all right, Rosie. You just fainted."

"It was the voice. It scared the shit out of me," she said, her voice as quiet as a mouse.

"Theo, would you get me a brandy, please?" Emery asked.

Theo stood. "Of course, Doctor."

"I've never heard anything so evil." Rosie removed the towel from her forehead and sat up.

Theo returned with the aperitif. "Here you go, Dr. Brennan."

"Thank you." Emery took the glass and handed it to Rosie. "Drink this."

She took a sip, made a face, and then downed the rest without taking a breath. She took a few deep breaths. "I'm okay. It just knocked me for a loop."

"Me too," Theo said. "I dropped the tray. It's all lies. I want to know—"

"Theo, did you know anything about that room and the equipment?" Joan interrupted.

Theo leaned against the wall, slid down, and hung their head. "Frankie brought out the box the day before yesterday with instructions to set it up in the little room behind the bar. I thought it was a music system."

Phyl squatted in front of Theo and put her hand on their knee. "Theo, who turned it on? Who played the message?"

"I did," they said. "It's remote-controlled. The instructions said to push the button after dinner when everyone was in the room." They looked up at Phyl. "I thought it was music," they repeated.

Phyl patted Theo's knee and stood. "I believe you, Theo."

"I don't think we should be so fast to swallow that story," Joan said over Phyl's shoulder.

Theo jumped up; their hands balled into fists. "It's the truth. I can prove it. I have the instructions, and the memory stick was labeled 'music to excite.'"

Emery let out a little laugh. "Well, it certainly did that."

Darcy, sitting at one of the small tables, suddenly stood. Her face was red, and her hands clenched into fists. "This is bullshit!"

Virgie collapsed into a chair across from Darcy. "The Knowly woman—or Knolles, Knowl—whatever the hell she calls herself has a lot of explaining to do in the morning." She used the sleeve of her sweater to wipe tears from her face. "Why would she do this? We don't even know her."

"Exactly," Joan said. "We must determine who this person is."

"Your Honor," Rosie spoke up from her place on the sofa, "would it be all right if I went upstairs to my room? I'd like to lie down."

"Of course, Mrs. Roberts." Joan smiled and looked at Theo. "Why don't you help your wife to your room, then come back down."

"Yes, ma'am," Theo said, helping Rosie to her feet.

After the two had left, Tamara flopped down on the vacant sofa. "I don't know about the rest of you, but I need a drink."

"Scotch?" Phyl asked.

Tamara nodded.

Phyl went behind the bar and grabbed a bottle of single malt and two crystal glasses. "Anyone else?"

All but Catherine and Emery raised a hand. Catherine shook her head. "Alcohol is the devil's drink," she muttered.

"I'll wait and have tea," Emery said.

"Okay." Phyl set four more glasses on the bar and poured the rich brown liquid into each glass. Willie picked up three glasses and handed one to Tamara and Virgie. Phyl picked up the other three, giving one to Joan and Darcy and keeping one for herself.

"Under normal circumstances, I'd say *sláinte*," Willie said.

"Sláinte?" Virgie asked.

"It's the Irish equivalent of cheers." Willie raised her glass. "My grandad used to say, 'May yer glass be ever full. May the roof over yer head be strong. And may ya be in heaven half an hour before the devil knows yer dead.'"

A few minutes later Theo reentered the room, holding a tray with a silver teapot and two teacups. They placed the tray on the table next to Catherine and poured tea into a cup.

"Theo, I'll have tea," Emery said.

"Yes, ma'am." Theo nodded and repeated the process.

"How was Rosie when you left her?" Emery asked.

"I think she'll be fine after a good night's rest." Theo placed the cup of tea on the small table in front of Emery.

"I'll check in on her before we retire. I can give her a sedative if she can't sleep."

"Thank you." Theo smiled slightly.

Using the tone she usually reserved for court, Joan took charge. "All right, now that we're all settled, let's get down to business. I think it's obvious that we weren't brought here for the reasons we were told."

Darcy slammed her glass down on the bar. "No, we were lied to and manipulated."

"Whoever it is, believes we've hurt other people," Phyl said.

"Or, in your case, killed other people." Willie folded her arms and leaned against the bar. "Is it true? Did you kill six schoolchildren?"

Phyl's shoulders sagged. "It was a horrible accident. I don't want to talk about it."

Joan cleared her throat. "Theo, who is this Knowles person?"

Theo stood frozen. Their eyes darted from one person to the next. "They own the place, ma'am."

"Do you know that for a fact?" She questioned Theo like a prosecutor would a hostile witness.

Theo clenched their jaw and took a deep breath. "How could I know that for sure?"

Joan scowled. "What did she say when she interviewed you?"

"She didn't. We've never actually met her. Mr. Moore interviewed us and made the arrangements to get here." Theo crossed their arms. "The only contact we've had with Ms. Knowles has been by letter or email."

Darcy piped up. "We don't know if it's a man or a woman or if Knowles is even their real name."

Joan nodded. "True," she said. "What about by phone or the CB radio?"

Theo exhaled slowly. "No. She's never called or texted. As I said, the only cell service is on the west side of the island, and that's only when the weather is good. She's never used the CB radio." Theo took a seat on the arm of the sofa. "We've only been here three days. The house was fully stocked when we arrived. Besides the instructions that came with the boxes Frankie brought over and an email, we haven't had any personal contact with Ms.—or Mr. Knowles."

Joan thought for a minute. "What was in the instructions?"

Theo took a deep breath and exhaled. "We were to prepare eight rooms for guests arriving on Friday and make the guests comfortable until she arrived. But this morning we received an email saying she'd been delayed."

Joan stared at Theo. "You said there's no Wi-Fi. How did you get an email?"

"Rosie and I have been walking around the island every morning. I check my phone when we're on the west side," they explained. "There's only been the one email."

"Show it to me," Joan demanded.

Theo pulled a phone out of their pocket.

"Why do you carry your phone if there's no service?" she asked.

Theo's face turned a light shade of pink. "Rosie and I take pictures and post them for our family when we can get a signal." Theo brought up the email and handed the phone to Joan.

"It's from a Gmail account. Any Tom, Dick, or Harry could make up a fake account," Joan said.

Darcy stood. "It seems at least five of us have a connection to the deaths of two little girls. But how?" She looked at Joan, Tamara, Emery, and Catherine.

"Those two girls were murdered by a man named Nicolas Shelton," Joan said from her seat at the bar. "He'd been accused of the murder of another little girl, but a mistrial was declared, and he was released pending the district attorney refiling the case." Joan swallowed the contents of her glass before continuing, "He killed them a few days after being released."

"Oh my God, I remember." The color drained from Darcy's face. "I testified in the court case." She pointed at Joan. "You were the judge."

Everyone looked at Joan. "Yes, and you were hired by the defense. You had some ridiculous story about the effects of childhood trauma on a person's ability to know right from wrong."

"That's not ridiculous. Childhood trauma can cause lasting cognitive impairment."

"So you say." Joan turned to Willie. "That's why you look so familiar. You were one of the officers who investigated the case."

Willie nodded. "I wondered if you knew who I was."

Joan looked across the room at Emery. "You also testified in Shelton's defense."

Emery nodded but didn't say anything. Joan looked at Tamara and then Catherine. "I have no idea how you two are connected to the case."

Catherine looked up from her Bible. "I was on the jury."

Tamara drained her glass. "I thought you looked familiar. I was on the jury also. I'd just turned eighteen." She got up and headed to the bar. "The worst experience of my life." She set her glass down on the mahogany surface and reached for the bottle of scotch, filling her glass halfway.

Joan ignored the comment. "So, five of us have a strange connection to a murder case."

"None of this makes any sense," Catherine said. "I was invited here for a Christian retreat."

"Who invited you?" Joan asked.

Catherine closed her Bible and turned to face the group. "I received a letter with a signature I couldn't read. It was supposedly from a woman I'd met several years ago at a Christian retreat. She said she had opened a similar retreat on the island and invited me to come here as her guest. I thought the name was Knott or Nottingham. I did know someone named Knott, and my grandmother's family name was Nottingham. I assumed it was either my old acquaintance or a distant cousin." She took a sip of her tea. "I'm sure I don't know anyone named Knowles or Knowly."

"A letter? Not an email?" Darcy asked.

"No, I don't do email. I don't even own a computer." She arched her back and squared her shoulders. "They're sinful."

Joan looked at Virgie. "And you?"

"I received a typed, certified letter signed by Mrs. Knowly. I still have it if you want to see it."

"Maybe later," Joan said. "Please continue."

"It was an offer of employment. To tutor her two children while they vacationed on the island. She said she'd gotten a recommendation from a past employer I don't remember ever working for."

In unison, Joan, Catherine, and Darcy said, "She has children?"

Virgie gulped down the remains of her scotch and handed the glass to Phyl. "Another, please."

Phyl took the glass and smiled at her. "Of course."

Virgie looked back at the others. "I don't know if she has children. That's what the letter said. But Rosie said they didn't know anything about children and don't have a room prepared for them."

Heads turned to look at Theo. "She's right. We weren't told there would be children."

Joan turned to Phyl. "And you, Ms. Long?"

Phyl glanced at Virgie, who nodded encouragement. "I was contacted in person by Mr. Moore. He said he represented Ms. Knowles. She wanted to hire me to ghostwrite a book about the island."

"Ghostwrite?" Catherine asked. "What is that?"

Phyl took a sip of her scotch before answering. "I write books for other people, celebrities and politicians mostly. They don't have the know-how to write it themselves."

"So, she wanted you to write a book, but it would have her name on it as the author?" Darcy asked.

"Yes. It's quite common. Few celebrities write their own books."

Tamara's head jerked up, her eyes wide. "What? You mean Kim Kardashian didn't write her own book?"

Phyl shook her head.

"Did you write it?" Tamara asked.

"I'm bound by contracts. I can't say who I've worked for." Phyl stretched her neck from side to side. "Sorry."

Tamara slumped back on the sofa and took a large swallow of her drink. Virgie put a hand to her mouth and suppressed a small laugh.

Darcy stood, shoved her hands into her pockets and looked at Joan. "As for me, I received an email from a Ms. Knolles, a secretary at NYU, where I was a psychology professor, doing research on trauma and its effects on the brain." She frowned. "I don't remember anyone there by that name. But secretaries come and go. The email said several retired professors were coming here to reconnect, and I was invited to join them."

Joan squinted. "You didn't think that was odd?"

Darcy collapsed onto her chair. "Looking back on it, I should have asked more questions. But at the time, I was happy that my colleagues wanted to include me. I hadn't heard from any of them for several years."

Joan turned to Emery. "And you, Dr. Brennan?"

"It was a house call of sorts. Like Virginia, I received a certified letter. It asked me to treat Mr. Knowles's wife. It described her symptoms, the treatment she'd already received, and a request that I take a look at her."

"You'd never had any contact with them before that?" Joan asked.

Emery shook her head. "Never."

Joan looked at Tamara, still sitting on the sofa, drink in hand. "Ms. Miller?"

"An email from a sorority sister. She said several of the girls were getting together here and asked if I could join them." She grimaced. "I didn't think twice about it not being real."

Joan continued her interrogation, looking directly at Willie. "That leaves you."

"As you know, I was a cop. Now, I do private security. Mr. Moore hired me to keep an eye on you." She looked at each person. "On all of you."

There was a sharp collective intake of breath. "What? Why?" Darcy and Theo asked in unison. Eight pairs of angry eyes waited for an answer.

Darcy, fists clenched, took a step toward Willie. "Start talking before I beat the shit out of you."

Willie smiled. "Did you not hear me say I was a cop? I can hold my own in a fight. On the other hand, you were a professor, probably ensconced behind a desk most of the time."

Darcy's face was red with anger. "I work out every day and run five miles. I'll bet the only thing you work out with is a bottle of scotch."

"I'll have you know—"

Emery stepped between them. "That's enough. Your bickering isn't helpful." She looked from Willie to Darcy.

"The doctor's right," Joan said. "Darcy, Willie, please take a seat so we can continue."

Darcy glared at Willie.

"Ms. Kerrel, how exactly were you hired? What exactly are your duties?"

Before speaking, Willie picked up her scotch, swallowed the remains and wiped her mouth with the back of her hand.

"Stop dragging your feet. Out with it," Joan demanded.

"All right, all right. Moore showed up at my office about a month ago with a check and a ticket for the ferry. He said Ms. Knowles was hosting an event at her home on Castaway Island

and needed security because she didn't know the people well. I was given a list of your names but no other information."

"I see." Joan turned to Phyl, who stood behind the bar. "Would you mind pouring me another scotch before we continue?"

"Sure. Anyone else?"

Willie handed Phyl her glass.

Phyl poured a small amount into the glass and pushed it back across the bar. Willie picked it up and took a large swallow. "I've spilled my guts. Now it's your turn, Judge Hathorne."

Phyl handed Joan her glass, and she took a sip, wincing as it burned her throat. "Yes, of course." She paused and took a breath. "Mr. Moore came to see me. He said Ms. Knowles was a wealthy conservative who donated a lot of money to political candidates with similar values. He said she wanted to talk to me about my running for Congress. He gave me a letter from her inviting me here to discuss it." Joan took another drink of her scotch and looked around the room. "So, we were all lured here under false pretenses, a few in-person by the mysterious Mr. Moore. Others by email or letter." She looked from face to face. Heads nodded in agreement. "Our host's name varies but always starts with K-N-O. Only a few give the first name, but those that do show it as Una or just U." She looked around again. "Does anyone see where I'm going with this?"

"I do," Phyl said. "When you put part of the first name, Un. And part of the last name, Kno, together…." She paused. "It's Unknown. Someone's playing a game with us."

"That's crazy!" Virgie jumped up. "Why is this happening?"

Joan nodded. "Yes, it is crazy. And whoever's behind this could be dangerous."

Emery took a deep breath. "Whoever it is has gone to a lot of trouble to find out about us. Who our friends are, our colleagues, our lovers?" She looked around the room at each person. "Our transgressions."

"But why?" Virgie asked, tears running down her face.

Phyl walked over from behind the bar and put a hand on her shoulder. "That's the million-dollar question."

"They're wicked. God will roast them in the fires of hell," Catherine said, clutching her Bible to her chest.

Tamara didn't say a word as she drained her drink. Willie rubbed the back of her neck, not looking directly at anyone.

Theo's face was beet red. "It's a lie. Rosie and I didn't do anything wrong."

Joan held up her hand for quiet. One by one, they turned to look at her. When she had everyone's attention, she put both hands in her pockets and looked directly at each one before speaking. "This person accused five of us in the death of two little girls who were murdered by Nicolas Shelton," she said. "The five of us were, in one way or another, involved in his first trial. I assume this person blames us for those two girls' deaths because the trial ended in a hung jury." She looked at Tamara, then Catherine. "The jury couldn't come to a unanimous decision, and I had to declare a mistrial and release him pending a new trial." Joan looked tired. Her shoulders sagged. "I didn't have a choice. I had to follow the rule of law."

Tamara's eyebrows raised. "You weren't very nice to the jury, Judge."

Joan waved her off. "I don't remember you." She took a sip from her glass. "In any case, trials aren't popularity contests. I had a job to do, and I did it."

Emery looked from Joan to Tamara and back at Joan. "I testified in that trial."

Joan huffed. "Yes, you did. You spun some absurd story about how his mother's schizophrenia affected his ability to understand right from wrong. Pure bullshit."

Emery stood and faced Joan, her fists clenched. "It's not bullshit. There are several peer-reviewed studies on the issue."

"Ludicrous is what it is. A made-up condition to excuse criminal behavior."

"I agree with the judge," Willie chimed in. "There was no doubt he killed that girl."

From her seat at the bar, Tamara said, "The prosecutor didn't prove the case. There were too many unanswered questions. We were split, six guilty, six not guilty."

Joan finished her scotch and set the glass back on the bar. "It was obvious to me."

Willie guffawed. "Yet you went ahead and declared a mistrial rather than make them continue to deliberate."

"It wouldn't have done any good," Tamara said. "We were never going to agree."

"It's terrible that he went out and killed those two girls," Emery said. "But no one wants an innocent person sent to prison for something they didn't do."

"Doctor, that rarely happens," Joan said.

Emery stared at the judge, dumbfounded at her callousness. "Even one person wrongfully convicted is one too many."

"Please, Doctor, spare me your bleeding-heart, liberal opinions. You have no idea how many evil people are out there, just waiting to make you their next victim."

"There's a lot of evil in the world. And the average person is oblivious to it," Willie offered.

"'Let those who love the Lord hate evil, for he guards the lives of his faithful ones and delivers them from the hand of the wicked.' Psalm 97:10," Catherine recited without looking up from her knitting.

"Oh God, spare me," Virgie mumbled.

Catherine nodded. "Yes, pray to God to spare you."

Virgie glared at the back of Catherine's head, then sat up straight, pushed her shoulders back, and looked at the others. "I'd like to tell you about the little boy, Kenneth. It was his obituary in the envelope."

Phyl sat in the chair beside her and put her hand on Virgie's knee. "You don't have to do that."

She gave Phyl a weak smile. "No, I need to." She paused briefly, gathering courage. "He was five years old. I was his nanny, just for the summer. The family had rented a beach house on the central coast of California. I had taken him to the beach early in the morning when the tide had gone out. We were going to explore the tide pools. It was a beautiful day. The sun was out. The sky was clear." She looked at Phyl, who reached over and took her hand. "We were having so much fun.

I can still hear him squeal each time we'd find a tiny crab or sand dollar." She swallowed, trying to hold off the sob rising in her throat. "He climbed a rock and was a few yards away from me looking for starfish. I only took my eyes off him for a second to take a picture. I don't even remember what it was."

Tears began to stream down her face. "I didn't see it, the sneaker wave. It came out of nowhere. One minute, the ocean was quiet and calm, then a roar so loud it was like a train barreling down on us. Later, bystanders told the authorities the wave was twenty feet tall. It rose up and grabbed us, pulling us out into the ocean." She looked at Phyl. "I fought as hard as I could to get to him, but it kept pulling me farther and farther away," she sobbed. "Kenny went under and never came back up. I lost consciousness. I remember waking up on the beach with the lifeguard over me. They didn't find his little body until the next day. It washed up two miles south of where we'd been." She leaned back in the chair, exhausted.

Phyl picked up the glass of scotch from the table and handed it to her. "Here, this may help," she said, putting a hand on Virgie's shoulder.

"Thank you," she whispered. Taking the glass, she gulped down its contents and then looked at the group. "I was cleared of any wrongdoing. The authorities called it a sneaker wave. They occur unexpectedly and without warning."

"But you *did* take your eyes off him," Willie pointed out.

Virgie's head shot up. "Only for a second to take a picture."

"An act of God. We are not meant to understand his will," Catherine said.

Virgie turned on her in a fury. "If that's what your God does, I don't want any part of it. He was an innocent child. No loving being would take him away like that."

"We must not—"

"Just shut the fuck up," Virgie yelled. "No one wants to hear that bullshit."

Catherine's eyes bulged to the size of dinner plates. "You are a sinner and surely on your way to hell. No wonder God punished you."

Emery jumped in front of Catherine. "That's enough. Stop it."

Joan agreed, "Catherine, that's not helpful."

Darcy walked up behind Virgie and patted her on the shoulder. "Ignore that hateful woman. Karma will deal with her."

After a minute of silence, Phyl stood and turned to face the others. "This sociopath that brought us here accused me of having caused the death of six children." Her face was red with anger. "Their obituaries were in the envelope." She swallowed a sob and then continued, "It was a horrible tragedy. A horrible accident." She closed her eyes as if gathering her strength. Once she opened them, she blinked several times. "It was ten years ago. I was driving from New York to Boston to meet with a client. It was freezing. The rain was turning to sleet. I hit a patch of black ice and spun out of control. My car crossed over the center divider. The school bus driver swerved out of the way, but she lost control. The bus went down an embankment and crashed into a tree." Tears streamed down Phyl's face. Virgie reached out and took her hand. "When my car came to rest on the side of the road, I jumped out and ran toward the bus. The driver had helped a few children out by the time I got there. Before I could help her, the bus exploded into a fireball. I was blown back thirty feet. I woke up in the hospital with third-degree burns on ten percent of my body. The police told me three kids survived, but the driver and six children didn't make it," she sobbed. "They didn't charge me. I wasn't speeding or driving recklessly. It was a horrible accident." She sat, lowered her head into her hands, and cried. Virgie put her arm across Phyl's shoulder and pulled her close.

Tamara stood up unsteadily. "This is bullshit. Who is making us relive these horrible events?" She swayed a little from side to side. "It's not right."

Emery handed her a glass of water. "Tamara, drink this. You'll thank me in the morning."

"Thanks, Doc." She took the glass and guzzled half of it.

Theo, who had been standing off to the side, cleared their throat. All heads turned to look. "I'd like to say something about what the voice accused Rosie and me of."

Emery nodded. "Go ahead, Theo."

They closed their eyes briefly. "In the envelope was Madeline Brady's obituary. Mrs. Brady was elderly and very frail. Her son hired us to be her live-in caretakers. We aren't nurses. Rosie has a nurse's aide certificate, and we both have CPR and first-aid training but no other medical training. Her son knew that. He just wanted us to tend to her needs. We cooked for her, cleaned the house, helped her bathe, and ensured she took her medication. You know that kind of stuff." They looked at Willie. "Ms. Kerrel, do you think I could have a shot of something to calm my nerves?"

Willie nodded. "Of course. Tequila?"

Theo nodded and turned back to the others. "I was only twenty-five, and Rosie was twenty-four. We took good care of her for two years. Before that, we'd worked in a nursing home for a year. Granted, we didn't have much experience, but we did right by her. One of us was always with her, day and night."

Willie walked up and handed Theo the shot glass of tequila and a wedge of lime. "Thank you." They swallowed the clear liquid, sucked on the lime, and winced at the taste. "The night she passed we were with her. There was a terrible storm. The power went out and her oxygen machine wouldn't work. I tried to call for help, but the landline was down and lightning had hit the nearby cell tower." Theo fought to hold back the sob that grew in their throat. "I carried Mrs. Brady to the car. I was going to take her to the hospital myself. But when I pushed up the garage door, the street was flooded. We couldn't get out." They began to cry. "I carried her back into the house and laid her on the sofa near the fireplace to keep her warm. An hour later, she died." Tears flowed down their face. "We tried, honest to God, we tried."

Except for Theo's sobs and the raging wind outside, it was quiet in the room until Catherine made a clicking sound with her tongue. "It is not up to us to question God's will. He has a greater plan that is not ours to know," she said, exchanging her Bible for her knitting.

Virgie jumped to her feet and glared at the older woman. "Bullshit!" She clenched her hands into fists. "Just shut up. Do you hear me? Just shut up! No one wants to hear it."

Catherine looked up in surprise. She gave Virgie a smirk. "God has a plan for each of us. You will see."

Virgie took a step toward Catherine. "I said shut—"

Darcy stepped in front of her and put a hand on her shoulder. "That's enough. It's not helping."

Unfazed, Catherine said, "Proverbs 29:22. 'One given to anger causes much transgression.'" She looked directly at Virgie. "Perhaps you were angry the day you let that innocent little boy die."

"Catherine, that's enough!" Joan shouted. Turning to Willie, she continued, "What about you?"

Willie took a sip of her scotch and stared at Joan. "What about me?"

"Don't play coy. You know what I'm asking. What was in the envelope?"

"If you must know, it was Timothy Button's obituary. He robbed half a dozen liquor stores." She took another sip of her scotch and added, "At gunpoint."

"Yes, I remember the case. It got a lot of press. You were the investigating officer."

"Yes, I was."

"The young man was only sixteen at the time?"

"Yes, and he was tried as an adult and found guilty of all six robberies and assault with a deadly weapon."

"If I remember correctly, I sentenced him to fifty years in prison."

Willie raised her chin and narrowed her eyes. "Yes, you did."

Joan paused before saying anything. "And another inmate killed him a year later. He'd just turned eighteen."

Willie swallowed the rest of her drink and stared at Joan before glancing at the others in the room. "I'm not responsible for what happens to them in prison. Buttons was a thug. He shot a security guard. That guard almost died."

"And you got a medal and a promotion," Joan clarified.

"I earned both," Willie sneered.

Joan tilted her head to the side. "Just before Buttons was killed, he'd been granted an appeal."

Willie stared menacingly at Joan. "On a bullshit technicality."

"No, it was a question of the evidence." Her eyes bore holes into Willie. "Evidence you collected."

Willie slammed the empty glass down on the bar. "I did what I needed to do to put the son of a bitch behind bars."

"That's why you were fired? Internal Affairs found out you mishandled evidence and lied under oath at the trial."

Willie's face turned crimson. "I wasn't fired!" A tiny bit of spittle flew out of her mouth. "I resigned. I got my pension."

Joan took a seat at the bar and turned slightly away. "And because of you, a sixteen-year-old boy, who may or may not have been guilty, went to prison and was murdered there."

Catherine put down her knitting needles and looked up. "The Bible says an eye for an eye."

"Oh, my God, you are such a freaking hypocrite!" Virgie said.

Catherine put a hand to her chest. "I have no idea what you mean."

"What about 'Turn the other cheek'? What about 'Love thy neighbor'? What about being merciful? What about forgiveness?"

Catherine let out a huff. "You are taking the Bible out of context."

"Really? I think, 'Love your neighbor as you would yourself,' is pretty clear."

"You don't know anything. You're a heathen and a fornicator. We've all seen how you are throwing yourself at Ms. Long. It's disgusting."

Virgie sat stunned, unable to respond.

"Now, wait a minute." Phyl glared at Catherine. "Virgie and I haven't done anything inappropriate. And if we had, we're both consenting adults. It's none of your business."

Virgie found her voice. "What about those two dead girls?" She leaned forward. "You don't seem too upset about them."

"It is not for us to question God's plan."

Virgie's mouth dropped open. "Your lack of empathy is astounding."

"Don't judge me, you child of Satan!" Catherine's face was flaming red.

Virgie laughed in her face. "You just proved my point. You need a name tag: Hypocrite for Jesus."

Catherine stood up and pointed a knitting needle at Virgie. "God will punish you for your heresy. Just you wait."

Darcy jumped in between them and held Catherine back. Emery took the twelve-inch needles away from her. "I'll keep these safe," she said.

"Proverbs 29:22. 'One given to anger causes much transgression,'" Virgie said with a mocking smile.

The room was silent until Joan cleared her throat. "Theo, does anyone else have a house on the island?"

Theo shook their head. "No, ma'am. This is the only one. There's a couple of storage sheds and a small garage, but that's it."

"So, no one else on the island except the ten of us?"

Theo nodded. "Nobody else. Just us."

Virgie choked down the sob rising in her throat. "I don't understand why someone would do this."

Tamara, unsteady on her feet, stood and headed for the bar. "Why? Because they think each of us caused someone's death or actually killed someone." She stopped and looked at Phyl. "Or six."

Phyl glared at her but didn't respond.

Tamara held up her empty glass. "I need a refill. Anyone else?" Her words were slightly slurred. Everyone shook their heads.

"Party poopers." She grabbed hold of the bar to keep from falling.

Emery held out a hand, ready to catch the inebriated woman if she fell. "Whoever this person is, they're unstable," Emery said.

"Unstable?" Virgie said sarcastically. "How about insane?"

Willie nervously shoved her hands in her pockets and paced to the end of the bar. "We have to leave the island." She looked up at the others. "The sooner the better."

"We can't," Theo said quietly as they collapsed onto a barstool.

Wrinkles creased Phyl's brow. "Why not?"

"There's no boat. There's no way off the island until Frankie comes back in the morning."

"Damn it." Willie slammed her hand on the bar.

"Who owns an island and doesn't keep a boat on it?" Joan demanded.

"Someone who doesn't want people to leave," Darcy said.

Virgie began to pace, then turned to Theo. "Can you radio her to come back tonight?"

Theo shook their head. "I already tried. It's not working. It's the weather. And even if it were working, the sea is too rough for the pontoon boat. It would be too dangerous."

Joan stood. "We should all get some sleep, if we can, and leave first thing in the morning. Theo, what time does Ms. Nugent usually arrive?"

"Between eight and nine a.m., depending on the weather."

"All right. I'll see you all in the morning."

Catherine stood and said, "I'm going to go to my room also."

Tamara raised her glass. "Sweet dreams," she slurred, then drained the glass and slammed it down on the bar with a thud and coughed…then coughed again. Her face turned red, and she gasped as she raised her hand to her throat and she dropped to her knees. Emery rushed to her, wrapped both arms around Tamara just below her breasts, and jerked forcefully several times. Nothing came up. Emery laid the now-unconscious woman on the floor, checked her airway, and then began pumping up and down on her chest. After a minute, sweat trickled down her forehead. Still, she continued until exhaustion forced her to stop. She stared at Tamara's lifeless body in disbelief.

CHAPTER FIVE

"She's dead." Emery's voice was barely audible. She closed her eyes. It happened so fast. In the blink of an eye, a vibrant, beautiful young woman lay dead at her feet. She looked at the others. Everyone stared at her, but no one spoke. Other than the sound of wind and rain thrashing against the house, the room was silent.

Then it sank in. Someone gasped. Virgie began to cry.

Catherine clutched her Bible and began to pray. "The Lord is our…" She didn't continue and stood staring at the body.

Darcy knelt next to Emery. "Dead? How? There wasn't any ice in her drink. How could she choke to death?"

Emery picked up Tamara's glass and held it to her nose. Her eyebrows raised. "She didn't choke." She held out the glass. "Theo, can you find me a sealable plastic bag to put this in?"

Theo stood there, frozen.

"Theo." Emery raised her voice.

"Of course." They nodded and headed for the kitchen.

"Doc, what's going on?" Phyl put her arm around Virgie and rubbed her back.

Before answering, Emery paused and chewed on her bottom lip. "There's a faint smell of almonds in the glass."

Virgie cocked her head. "Scotch doesn't smell like almonds."

"No, it doesn't." Emery placed the glass in the plastic bag Theo handed her. "But prussic acid does."

"Prussic acid? What's that?" Catherine asked, still clutching her Bible.

"Its common name is cyanide. It kills almost instantly."

"Where did it come from?" Catherine asked.

"I have no idea," Emery said. "It occurs naturally in nature. It can be made from chokecherries and Johnsongrass." She walked over to the bar, picked up the bottle of scotch, and held it to her nose. "Nothing. It wasn't in the bottle."

Virgie looked startled. "So, it was put in her glass between the bar and the sofa?"

Willie turned to Emery. "Did she kill herself?"

"I doubt anyone would kill themselves with cyanide. It's a horrible way to die."

Virgie looked up at Emery. "I can't believe she'd kill herself. She was so young, so full of life." She shook her head. "No, she wouldn't do that."

"The alternative is that someone else put the poison in her glass," Emery said.

Everyone silently looked from one to another. Phyl was the first to speak. "Let's not jump to conclusions. There's no reason to suspect she was murdered." She turned to Theo. "Can you try the CB radio again?"

"I tried when I went to get the bag for the doctor." They shrugged. "There's just static."

"Okay. First thing in the morning, we'll try again. If we still can't get through to them, we'll take her body back with us on Frankie's boat."

"If the storm clears and she's able to get out here," Theo interjected.

Phyl nodded. "Yes. If she's able to get out here."

Emery stood. "We can't leave her here. The body will become quite unpleasant by morning."

Virgie pointed to the room behind the bar. "I'll get a blanket."

"Why don't we carry her up to her room?" Willie suggested.

"I'll help you," Darcy volunteered.

After wrapping the body in the blanket, Willie and Darcy easily lifted Tamara's body off the floor.

It was after midnight when they returned to the front room. The others were still present but they'd let the fire go out, and a chill invaded the space.

Emery stood. "We should all get some sleep."

"I agree," Joan said. "Even if Mrs. Knowles arrives in the morning, I don't plan on staying."

Heads nodded.

"I have to finish cleaning the kitchen and getting things ready for breakfast," Theo said.

"All right," Joan said, then turned to Emery. "Dr. Brennan, would you mind checking on Rosie?"

"Of course. I'll give her a mild sedative if she hasn't fallen asleep."

"Thank you, I appreciate it. When I'm done here, I'll double-check to make sure everything is locked up tight."

"Okay. Good night, Theo," Emery said and followed the others up the stairs, the wood creaking with each step. *No one's going to be sneaking up or down these stairs.* As she climbed the stairs to the servants' quarters on the third floor, she was not surprised to hear locks being turned on six guest room doors.

Phyl and Virgie silently walked up the stairs, their shoulders touching. When they got to the end of the hall, Virgie put her key in the lock, opened the door, and turned to Phyl. "I don't think I'll be able to sleep."

Phyl took her hand. "Maybe a hot bath would help."

"Maybe."

"If you still can't sleep, knock on my door, and we'll talk." Phyl leaned down and kissed her cheek. "Good night," she said, then walked across the hall to her own room.

Joan stood at the open window and noticed the smell of rain in the air as she blew smoke out the window. She didn't care that the rooms were designated "nonsmoking." Rules didn't apply to judges. Judges were like gods. They enforced the rules; they punished those who broke them. They were elite, superior beings. The rules were for the lower classes and the riffraff.

Staring out into the black night, Nicolas Shelton came to mind. She remembered the young man vividly. With his blond hair, blue eyes, movie star smile, and straight white teeth, he'd charmed the jury with his "boy next door" good looks, but Joan hadn't been fooled. She was above that kind of thing. The more he'd tried to charm her, the more she detested him.

The prosecutor, Thomas Kincaid, had made a poor showing. His cross-examination had been overzealous, which had offended the jury. On the other hand, Shelton's attorney, Erin Mathews, had been outstanding, better than she expected from a public defender. She'd painted a picture of Shelton as a lost, misunderstood soul. He'd been abused as a child and placed in foster care, where his foster father sexually abused him. She'd put Shelton on the stand, and when he recounted the abuse he'd suffered at the hands of the very people who were supposed to keep him safe, two female jurors broke down in tears. Afterward, Ms. Mathews walked out of the courtroom like a peacock, strutting about like she owned the place. It had infuriated Joan.

It had been one of the more interesting cases she'd heard in the twenty years she'd been on the bench. She remembered sitting high up on her perch, looking down, judging everyone in attendance: the attorneys, the jury, the court staff, those in the gallery watching the proceedings, and, of course, Nicolas Shelton. But the jury hadn't been paying attention. They hadn't seen what she had, and they couldn't agree on his guilt. She had no choice but to let him walk out of the courtroom.

She shook her head, stubbed out her cigarette in a plant near the window, tossed the butt outside, and crawled into bed.

Emery lay in bed staring at the ceiling, the book she'd tried to read abandoned next to her. Thoughts of Nicolas Shelton and the little girls he'd killed filled her head. It was such a tragedy.

She rolled over and placed the book on the nightstand, turned the light off, and closed her eyes. She quickly opened them when Tamara Miller's lifeless body appeared behind her eyelids. She wished she still drank. A Valium would help her sleep, but drugs were out of the question. She'd been clean too many years to give in to that temptation. She hadn't taken any pharmaceuticals or consumed alcohol since she'd performed surgery on Louise Carpenter and killed her all those years ago. Her drug use had started innocently enough in med school. A pill every now and then to relieve her anxiety before big exams. It had been easy to buy them from other students who sold their prescription medications to make a little money on the side. That led to buying Adderall to stay awake during long study sessions. By the time she'd graduated, she was addicted.

Virgie paced back and forth across her room, stopping to stare out the open window into the black night sky. Unable to quiet her mind, she thought about the events of the night. Things hadn't gone quite the way she'd imagined the first night on the island. Putting a hand to her cheek, she thought about the kiss Phyl had placed on it. She took a deep breath and wished she'd asked the doctor for something to help her sleep. Turning from the window, she looked at the poem on the dresser.

"Ten little castaways went out to dine;
One choked her little self, and then there were Nine."

Tamara had died in a similar manner. Darcy had suggested the young woman committed suicide. Virgie shook her head. She couldn't imagine wanting to die. As bad as her life had been after Kenny's death and her near drowning, she'd never felt that she wanted to end her own life.

Darcy lay on her back, staring at the ceiling, listening to the wind whip through the trees outside her window. She'd tossed from side to side for the past hour, unable to sleep, her thoughts drifting to the Nicolas Shelton case and her testimony.

She stared out the window at the pitch-black sky. For some reason tonight's events stirred up memories of Robby Lindle. She'd liked the young man; he'd been an outstanding teaching assistant, and she'd enjoyed being a mentor and advisor on his dissertation. Both she and her husband had grown fond of him. Her husband had grown a little too fond of him. She'd come home from school early one afternoon and found them in bed together. She and her husband were both bisexual. She knew he was attracted to men. But finding out he was having an affair with her student was a shock. Without a sound, she'd closed the door and left the house. They had been so wrapped up in each other that they had never known she'd been there.

She never confronted her husband or Robby. A week later, at the dissertation hearing, she voted with the majority to deny his Ph.D. She could have fought for him. She probably could have convinced enough members to pass him. Since she was his advisor, they would have given weight to it if she thought he deserved it. But she didn't. Why would she? He had betrayed her.

The next night, Robby was dead. She managed to cry at his funeral; colleagues would have thought it odd if she hadn't. Her husband had sobbed. She never told him what she'd seen, and they continued on as before. A year later, at the age of fifty-five, her husband suffered a massive heart attack and died. That had been five years ago.

At the other end of the hall, Catherine, in her pink flannel nightgown, knelt next to her bed, her hands pressed together. Her Bible lay open in front of her, and she read Psalms 9:17 out loud. "'Death is the destiny of all the wicked, of all those who reject God. The needy will not always be neglected; the hope of the poor will not be crushed forever. Come, Lord! Do not let anyone defy you.'"

Across the hall from Virgie, Phyl sat on her bed, her back against the headboard, legs extended out in front of her, and her laptop on her lap. She thought it would be a good idea to write some notes about what had occurred today, starting with seeing Virgie on the ferry and ending with Tamara's death. It had all the makings of a murder mystery novel. She wondered how much money she'd make if she wrote under her own name. Being a ghostwriter meant letting other people take credit for her work. With each bestseller she wrote for someone else, the frustration grew.

Downstairs, Theo finished clearing the table and washing the dishes. As they went to turn off the light, they glanced at the miniature castaways on the shelf. One was missing. Not thinking much about it, they hurried up the stairs and quietly entered their room. Rosie lay sound asleep in the bed. Theo stood over her and smiled, then leaned down and kissed her on the forehead.

CHAPTER SIX

Early Saturday Morning

Emery was in the middle of a nightmare. Someone was pounding on a door, demanding to be let in. But let in where? Where was she? The knocking grew louder, more demanding.

She awoke with a start. It was morning, and the sun was up, but the pounding on her door continued. She jerked upright, reached for her robe, and stumbled to the door. It was Theo. They were in distress, panicked.

"Theo, what is it?"

"It's Rosie. She won't wake up. I don't think she's breathing." Tears rushed down their face. "Hurry, you have to help her." Theo turned and sprinted down the hall and up the stairs to the third floor. Taking a second to make sense of what Theo had said, Emery glanced out the window. The storm had paused, and the sun was creeping over the horizon. Shaking herself, she grabbed her medical bag and ran to the stairs and up to the Roberts' bedroom. When she entered, Theo was sitting on the bed, holding Rosie's hand, sobbing.

Emery put her hand on Theo's shoulder. "Let me sit so I can look at her."

Theo kissed Rosie's lifeless hand, gently placed it on the bed, and stood. Emery took their place on the bed and put the fingers of her right hand on Rosie's neck, feeling for a pulse. There wasn't one, and her skin was cold to the touch. She'd been dead for some time.

Emery removed a small feather from Rosie's hair then pulled the bedsheet over her face. She looked at Theo. "I'm so sorry, Theo, but she's gone."

"But…but…." Theo's knees buckled, and they melted to the floor, sobbing.

Emery knelt next to them and put a hand on their shoulder. "Theo, I'm so sorry." Theo continued to cry; deep, racking sobs of grief poured out.

Emery waited; when Theo had worn themself out, Emery asked, "Theo, when you came up last night, was Rosie awake?"

Theo shook their head. "No, she was sound asleep. I didn't want to wake her, so I went back downstairs and slept in the front room."

"And this morning?"

"I came up here to wake her so we could start breakfast." Theo wiped tears from their face with the sleeve of their shirt. "She wouldn't wake up."

"When you found her, were her eyes open or closed?"

Wrinkles creased Theo's forehead as they thought for a second. "Closed. Why? Is it important?"

"I don't know." Emery pulled the sheet from Rosie's face and opened one of her eyelids. The whites of her eye were streaked with red. She replaced the sheet and looked at Theo. "Did your wife have any health issues?"

"No, nothing medical." Theo shook their head. "She had a nervous condition and used to take medication for anxiety, but she'd been much better. She stopped taking it a few months ago."

"So, no heart trouble, no breathing issues?"

"No, nothing. She was healthy."

Emery rubbed her forehead and again thought about the Valium in her medical bag. "I hate to ask, Theo, but what about other drugs?"

Theo looked at Emery, not understanding what she meant. "She'd take aspirin occasionally for a headache or Motrin when it was her time of the month."

Emery stood. "Sorry, Theo, I meant, did she use any recreational drugs."

Theo was instantly angry. "Are you kidding? My wife just died, and you accuse her of being a drug addict?" Theo pounded their fist on the floor. "How dare you. I can't believe you could think something like that."

Emery raised her hands out in front of her. "Theo, I didn't mean any offense. I wasn't accusing her or you of anything. I'm just trying to figure out what happened."

Theo deflated like a spent balloon. They looked at Rosie's lifeless form on the bed. "As far as I know, the only drug she took was the one you gave her last night to help her sleep."

Emery's forehead wrinkled. "Theo, I didn't give her anything last night. She was sound asleep when I checked in on her. I checked her vital signs, then left."

Theo knelt at the side of the bed and took Rosie's lifeless hand in theirs. They began to cry again. "Then what happened? Why is she dead?"

Emery thought about the redness in Rosie's eyes but didn't give voice to her thoughts. "I have no idea, Theo. We need to contact the authorities and get them out here."

Without looking away from Rosie's body, Theo said, "Give me a few minutes, and I'll be down and call them on the CB."

Emery placed her hand on Theo's shoulder. "I'm deeply sorry, Theo. I wish I had answers."

Theo said nothing.

"I'll go downstairs and tell the others. We should all be ready to leave when the boat gets here." As she turned to leave, she noticed a small piece of paper sticking out from under the bed. She bent and picked it up. Her face fell when she read it. "Theo, you need to see this." She handed them the scrap of paper.

There were two words written on it in block letters. *I'm sorry.* Theo's face turned ashen. "What does this mean? Why would she say she's sorry?"

"Theo, would she have hurt herself?"

Theo's mouth opened, but no sound came out. They just stood there, staring at the body under the sheet.

After dressing quickly, Emery hurried down the staircase. She could see Joan pacing back and forth outside on the terrace, smoking a cigarette. She shook her head and pursed her lips. *Typical. She doesn't think the rules apply to her.* She found the others standing around the dining room, waiting for breakfast and discussing Tamara Miller's death.

As soon as Virgie saw Emery, she said, "Phyl and I were up at first light. We took advantage of the break in the storm and hiked to the west side of the island. We couldn't get cell service on either of our phones."

"And, no sign of the boat," Phyl added.

Darcy sat at the table with a huff. "And the coffee's not made. Has anyone seen Theo or Rosie?"

Emery steeled her resolve before she shared the news. "Please, everyone, have a seat. I have an announcement to make. Willie, would you ask the judge to join us?"

Willie nodded and headed for the front door. When she returned with Joan, Emery motioned for everyone to take a seat. She cleared her throat. "I have some difficult news to share."

Willie jumped up, her fists clenched. "If you tell us the boat isn't coming, I'm going to lose it, and I can't be held responsible for what might happen!"

"Is that it? Did Theo get through to the mainland on the radio? Is the boat not coming?" Virgie asked.

Emery shook her head. "Willie, please calm down. No one wants to stay here a minute longer than we must."

"Then what is it?" Willie said, reclaiming her seat at the table.

"I'm afraid Rosie Roberts passed away last night," Emery said, her hands clasped together on the table.

There was a sharp intake of breath from Virgie. Several seconds passed, then Catherine pulled her Bible out of her purse and began reading, "'But as for the cowardly, the faithless, the detestable; as for the murders, the sexually immoral, sorcerers, idolaters, and all the liars, their portion will be in the lake that burns with fire—'"

Virgie jumped up. "Stop it! That's enough. What's wrong with you? No one wants to hear that shit. A young woman is dead and you condemn her? You didn't even know her."

Catherine gave Virgie the same cold smile she had given her the night before. "Her fainting last night after the voice accused her and her partner of neglecting an old woman in their care, causing her death, is all I need to know," Catherine said smugly. "Guilt. It was her guilt that killed her."

"Unbelievable," Virgie said. "You are such a bitch."

Catherine sat up straight and raised her chin. "I beg your pardon. I am a faithful follower of Christ."

"No, you are a hypocrite," Virgie said as she pushed her chair back. "I can't stand to be in the same room with you. I'm going to make coffee," she said as she stormed from the room.

The others sat silently, unsure what to say about Catherine's judgmental attitude, lack of empathy, or Virgie's anger.

Finally, Phyl stood. "I think I'll see how I can help in the kitchen," she said as she hurried from the room.

"I'll give them a hand," Darcy said, making a quick exit.

Emery turned to Catherine. "Was that necessary?"

Catherine crossed her arms. "I only spoke God's words. His will be done."

Joan looked at Catherine. "It was a very uncharitable thing to say."

Willie laughed out loud. "You're one to talk about being uncharitable. I didn't realize you were such a hypocrite."

Anger flashed across Joan's face. "Excuse me?"

"You relished being called 'the hanging judge.'" Willie made quotation marks in the air with her fingers. "You took joy in punishing people."

"I only meted out punishment to those who were guilty of crimes. It was my job."

"And you took immense pride in it," Willie added. "I'm sure the doctor would agree with me. She was in your courtroom often enough."

Joan glared across the table at Emery.

Emery raised her hands. "I'm not going to get in the middle of this."

Joan turned back to Willie. "What's wrong with taking pride in your work?" she fired back. "Didn't you take pride in being a cop? Until you were fired for your unethical behavior anyway."

Willie's face reddened. "You bitch. I told you last night I resigned. I wasn't fired." She pounded a fist on the table, rattling the small bowl of sugar. "And I only did what I did to stop a fucking criminal from hurting anyone else."

Emery stood and raised her hands. "Okay, okay, stop it. None of this is helping us get off the island."

Joan straightened her shoulders. "You're right, of course." She paused. "Has Theo attempted to contact Nugent on the radio?"

"No, they haven't come downstairs yet. And I'm not sure how much help Theo will be considering what happened."

Willie looked at Emery. "She was so young. It's just tragic. Any idea how she died?"

Emery decided not to say anything about the redness in Rosie's eyes, a sign of asphyxiation. "No. An autopsy will have to be done when we get back to the mainland." Emery exhaled. "But I found a scrap of paper on the floor that had the words, 'I'm sorry' written on it."

"Suicide is a mortal sin," Catherine mumbled.

Willie glared at her and turned back to Emery. "Was it suicide?"

"I have no idea. Theo said she was in good health and didn't use recreational drugs." She shrugged. "An autopsy will have to be done to determine the cause of death."

"Fuck," Willie sighed. "I've got to get off this island."

"We've all got to get off the island," Joan added.

"Yes, you're right." Willie nodded. "Maybe I can figure out the CB radio. It can't be that different from the police radio I had in my unit."

"That would be helpful. I think I saw it on the kitchen counter near the back door," Emery said.

Willie stood. "I'll go try."

Joan and Emery nodded. Willie passed Virgie carrying a coffeepot and Phyl holding a tray of coffee cups.

"Thank God," Joan said as Phyl placed an empty cup in front of her and Virgie filled it.

"You can thank us; we made the coffee, not God," Virgie said in all seriousness.

"Yes, of course. Thank you both."

Phyl continued around the table and placed a cup in front of Emery; Virgie followed behind her and filled each one. When she arrived at Catherine's seat, she set the pot of coffee in front of her and walked away, not offering to pour it for her as she had the others.

Catherine stood. "I prefer tea. I'll get it myself," she said and left the room.

Virgie took her seat at the table. "I can't believe two people are dead." She looked at Emery. "Could Theo have done something to her and left the note to make it look like a suicide?"

Emery again thought about the redness in Rosie's eye and then remembered the feather she'd removed from Rosie's hair. It had to have come from a pillow, but she wasn't ready to accuse Theo of murdering their wife. "Why would you think that? Do you know something the rest of us don't?"

"No. I just got a strange vibe from her yesterday. She was nervous. Or maybe it was fear. Maybe she was afraid of something or someone." She took a sip of her coffee. "Maybe Theo was abusive."

"That's a lot of maybes," Emery said as Darcy returned from the kitchen with two large plates: one piled high with toast, bagels, croissants, and the other with butter, cream cheese, strawberry jam, and several kinds of cheese.

She placed them on the buffet against the wall. "Breakfast is serv...Oh my God."

"What's wrong?" Virgie asked.

Darcy's face had gone white. "Two of the castaways are missing. There's only eight here."

Joan stood, almost knocking over her cup of coffee. "What kind of sick game is someone playing with us?"

Willie walked out of the kitchen with a stack of small plates and placed them on the table next to Phyl. Catherine followed with her cup of tea.

"I'm afraid I have bad news," Willie said.

"Fuck. Haven't we had enough of that for one day?" Virgie placed her elbow on the table and rested her head on the heel of her hand.

"The sun has only been up for two hours. What else can go wrong?" Phyl asked, placing a plate in front of herself and handing the rest to Joan.

"Don't ask. Don't give this goddamned madman any more ideas," Virgie said.

"The CB's broken." Willie put her hands on her hips. "I think it's been tampered with."

Everyone, except Catherine, stopped what they were doing and stared at Willie.

"What do you mean?" Joan demanded.

Willie walked over to the coffeepot and poured coffee into an empty mug. "There's no juice. It's dead. The outlet works, a small clock is plugged into it, and it's running." She went to the buffet and picked up a piece of toast. "Hey, there's only eight little castaways. Where's the other two?"

"We were just getting to that," Emery said.

Virgie looked around the table and said what everyone was thinking. "Theo was down here alone last night after we all went upstairs." She took a sip of her coffee.

"And they could've come down here and taken the second one while we were on our walk," Phyl volunteered.

"Why would Theo do that?" Emery asked.

Virgie shrugged. "Maybe Theo *is* Ms. Knowles, and they brought us here for some sick, twisted reason only they understand."

"Come on, enough with the maybes," Emery said. "Do you really think Theo would kill their own wife?"

"Maybe." Virgie stared at Emery. "They did cause that old woman's death, and Theo was afraid Rosie was going to admit to it."

Before anyone could respond, Theo walked into the room. They looked like hell, drained of color, eyes red and swollen. "I'm sorry about break...I'm sorry about breakfast. Can I get anyone anything?"

"No, Theo, of course not. We're fine. Please have a seat," Emery said, gesturing to the chair Tamara had sat in the previous night.

Theo hesitated. "Are you sure? I'm not one of the guests."

"I don't think any of us are here for the reasons we originally thought," Joan said. "We've all been lured here for some sick, twisted game."

"Theo, I'm so sorry for your loss. Rosie seemed like a lovely person," Phyl said.

A sob escaped from deep inside Theo. "She was. She was the sweetest person on Earth."

Darcy reached over and placed her hand on Theo's. No one knew what to say.

"Theo, I'm sorry to ask, but shouldn't the boat be here by now?" Darcy looked at her watch. "It's almost nine."

Theo wiped their face with a napkin and blew their nose. "She's usually here by eight if the weather's good. If she can't make it, she sends someone else."

"She's late," Catherine huffed, taking a sip of her tea. Silence filled the room.

An hour later, Phyl and Willie stood on the terrace, looking out at the ocean. The sun was out, but dark clouds were forming on the horizon.

"It looks like we're in for more bad weather," Phyl said.

"I don't want to be stuck here in a storm," Willie said. "What the hell happened to Frankie and the boat?"

Phyl shoved her hands into her pants pockets and sighed. "I don't know. Either she was told not to come, or something happened to her, or the boat, and she couldn't come. And without the radio, she can't contact us."

"I would think she'd contact the Coast Guard if she suspected a problem. Ask them to check on us?"

"That's why I'm leaning toward her being told she didn't need to come out here today," Phyl said. "I hate to think something happened to her."

Willie collapsed onto a lounge chair. "I don't think she's coming. Not today and not tomorrow. The fucker who brought us here made sure of it. This whole thing's a shit show, don't you think? Two women are dead. What the hell is going on?"

"That's a good question." Phyl cracked her knuckles. "And while we're asking questions, is there a Mrs. Knowles? And if there is, why did she bring ten strangers here?"

Joan walked out onto the terrace, an unlit cigarette in her fingers. "We're not all strangers. Willie, Emery, and I know each other through the courts." She lit the cigarette. "I wouldn't be surprised if we were all somehow connected."

Phyl's forehead showed several wrinkles. "What? Like Seven Degrees of Kevin Bacon?"

Joan frowned. "Who's Kevin Bacon?"

Phyl shook her head. "Never mind."

Joan exhaled smoke into the air. "My guess is the person who brought us here is going to pick us off one by one." She used her hand like a gun and fired pretend bullets. Without another word, she strode down the path to the cliffs.

"That was strange." Willie looked at Phyl. "Nobody killed Rosie. There was a note. It was a suicide. Wasn't it?"

"I thought so."

"I don't want to believe Theo killed her."

"Me either." Phyl rubbed the back of her neck. "The bigger question is, did someone murder Tamara, or did she poison herself."

"I can't see someone taking cyanide to kill themself." Willie cocked her head to the side.

Phyl put her hands in her pockets and looked at the ground. "If she didn't then Joan may be right. Someone killed them and isn't finished."

CHAPTER SEVEN

Saturday Morning

Much to her dismay, Virgie found herself in the kitchen when Catherine walked in with her teacup. She placed it in the sink and faced Virgie.

"That woman who brought us here yesterday. The one without a leg."

Virgie took a deep breath and stared at the ceiling. "You mean Frankie?"

"Yes. She seemed reliable, didn't she? Even missing a leg, she seemed like she could do the job. But I guess driving a boat isn't that difficult, even for a one-legged woman."

Virgie lowered her eyes and silently counted to five. "Yes, she seemed dependable and good at her job."

"Then where is she? Why is she late? I want to leave."

"We all want to leave, Catherine. Hopefully, she'll be here soon."

"I need some fresh air. I don't think it's safe to go alone."

Virgie stared at the woman. Her forehead wrinkled. "Are you asking me to go with you?"

"Yes. If it isn't too much trouble."

Virgie wanted to ask the woman if she was out of her fucking mind but didn't have the energy. "Sure," she said without enthusiasm.

After grabbing their raincoats, they headed for the west side to watch for the boat. The intense winds that had been so overpowering the night before had settled into a strong breeze. The ocean had calmed some. Small whitecaps appeared and quickly fell back into the icy blue-gray water. In the distance, dark, angry clouds approached.

There weren't any boats in sight, and Nantucket was too far away to see, even if they'd had binoculars.

Catherine was the first one to break the silence. "I can't believe I fell for that letter. How could I be such a fool?" she asked, not looking at Virgie.

"Don't feel too bad. We all fell for the ruse. She manipulated us like a pro."

"But for what purpose?"

"I'm afraid to consider the reasons." Virgie paused, then asked, "Do you think Theo killed Rosie, and they caused that woman's death?"

"Absolutely. The way Rosie fainted and Theo dropped the tray of coffee and tea at the sound of the voice?" Catherine turned her head and looked at Virgie. "The reactions of a guilty person."

"So, if it's true that they caused that woman's death, what about the accusations about the rest of us? Are they all true too?"

"Hmm, good question," Catherine said. She turned back to the sea. "Well, Ms. Long admits to causing the death of six schoolchildren."

"But it was an accident. She didn't mean to kill anyone."

"So, it would seem. I mean, look at the judge. She was only doing her job. It was her duty to punish sinners."

Virgie looked at Catherine, disbelief on her face. "I thought it was a judge's duty to hold criminals accountable for their crimes."

Catherine gazed out at the ocean. "Same thing."

The two stood silently looking at the ocean for several minutes, lost in their own thoughts.

"A few years ago, my mother fell down the basement stairs and broke her neck. The light wasn't working, and it was dark."

Virgie's eyes went wide. "That's terrible. I'm so sorry for your loss."

"She tripped over a sack of cat food I left on the seventh step."

"You left it on the seventh step?"

Catherine nodded. "The number seven has great significance in the Bible."

Virgie stared at her. "Did you leave it there on purpose?"

"Yes. Seven is my lucky number."

"It wasn't lucky for your mother."

Catherine shrugged. "You reap what you sow." She continued to stare at the increasingly turbulent ocean. "She violated the Ten Commandments." Her voice was flat, emotionless. "She fornicated with one of my father's deacons in the church." She made a clicking noise with her tongue. "He died in a car crash a few weeks later." She paused. "His obituary and the two murdered girls' obits were in the envelope with my name on it."

Virgie took a sharp intake of breath. "You killed him. And your mother?"

Catherine gave Virgie a smile that didn't reach her eyes. "It was God's will. Leviticus 20:10 says the man that commits adultery with another man's wife, both the adulterer and the adulteress, shall surely be put to death."

Virgie took a step away from the woman. "You killed them."

Catherine returned her gaze to the ocean. "Don't be ridiculous. Her sinful behavior caused her death. If she hadn't given in to temptation, it wouldn't have happened." Her voice didn't reflect any self-doubt or emotion. Not one shred of remorse.

Disgusted, Virgie turned and walked away, unable to stomach one more minute with the self-righteous woman who was no more a follower of Christ than Attila the Hun.

On the way back to the house, Virgie came across Darcy standing near the cliff's edge, close to where the stairs came up from the dock. Out in the ocean, the storm continued to brew. Dark, rolling clouds churned and whirled as they moved steadily closer to shore.

Virgie stood half a step further back from the edge. "Standing so close to the edge makes me nervous."

Darcy didn't turn to look at the other woman. "Heights don't bother me."

"Any sign of Frankie and the boat?" Virgie asked.

"No. I think she was told not to come."

"Why?"

"So, we'd be stranded out here. Defenseless." She paused. "We're sitting ducks."

"You think someone wants to harm us?"

Darcy looked at her. "We haven't been here twenty-four hours, and two people are dead."

Virgie's eyebrows scrunched together. "It's bizarre, I'll give you that."

"And is it just a coincidence that the castaways in the poem died the same way?"

Virgie frowned. "I don't know."

"Well, I, for one, don't believe in coincidences."

The two stood staring out to sea for a few minutes until Virgie asked, "Is it just me, or is there something deeply wrong with Catherine?"

Darcy let out a small laugh. "You mean other than her being a psycho religious nutjob?"

"So, I'm not the only one worried about her mental stability?"

Darcy shook her head. "No, I think we're all on the same page on that. Except maybe the judge. She seems willing to give Catherine the benefit of the doubt."

"She all but admitted to me that she killed her mother and the man her mother had an affair with."

Darcy's head whipped around to look at Virgie. "What?"

"Catherine takes no responsibility. She actually said it was God's punishment for her sinful behavior."

"So much for 'Christian charity' and 'love thy neighbor.'"

"She doesn't feel one ounce of regret or guilt. The woman is a cold-hearted bitch."

Darcy turned back to the ocean. "Something is definitely wrong with that woman."

"I know it's terrible to say, but it's too bad she wasn't the one who didn't wake up this morning," Virgie said.

"Exactly what I was thinking."

Virgie pulled her jacket tight around her. The wind had increased, and the dark clouds had moved closer to the island. "I'm going up to the house and get warm. I'll see you at lunch."

Darcy didn't look at her, keeping her eyes on the approaching storm. "Maybe," she said. "I'm not very hungry."

As Virgie approached the house, she found Phyl, Willie, and Emery seated on the terrace, talking. Judge Hathorne sat off by herself, smoking and seeming not to care about where the ash from her cigarette fell.

"You know there's no smoking here, don't you?" asked Virgie.

Joan laughed out loud. "We've been lured here by an unknown individual playing a bizarre game with us. Do you really think there are any rules?"

Virgie paused. "You have a point," she said as she headed for the door. As she passed by the others, Phyl waved to her.

"Virgie, come have a seat."

She shook her head. "I'm going to go to my room and lie down until lunch is ready." She paused. "Is Theo making lunch, or should we make our own?"

"Theo's making something. They said they needed to stay busy," Willie volunteered.

"Okay. I'll be in my room if anyone needs me."

Phyl smiled. "We'll talk after lunch?"

Virgie nodded and continued inside.

Phyl turned her attention back to the other two women. They were smiling at her. "What?" Phyl asked.

"It looks like the two of you have become friends," Willie said.

"I'd say a little more than friends," Emery teased.

"Pull your minds out of the gutter. We've only talked," Phyl said.

Emery held up her hands. "No judgment here. You're both adults."

"Thank you. Now, can we get back to that matter at hand?"

"Yes, of course," Willie said. "What's your take on the voice and the purpose for bringing us here?"

"Obviously, it has something to do with the deaths of the people mentioned in the recording. But why? What's his connection to them?" Phyl asked.

Emery leaned forward. "What makes you think it's a man? It could be a woman. Most of the letters and emails were signed by Ms. or Mrs."

"You're right," Phyl said. "We have no idea who we're dealing with or what they intend to do."

Willie stood up and stretched her back. "Doc, was Tamara poisoned?"

Emery leaned back in her lounge chair. "As I said last night, there was the scent of almonds in Tamara's glass."

"Was Rosie's death suicide?" Willie asked.

Emery looked at her questioningly. "I don't know. The only thing that suggests that is the slip of paper. But honestly, we don't know if she wrote it."

"Maybe she couldn't live with the guilt that they couldn't keep the old woman alive when the power went out," Phyl said.

"Or Virgie's right, and Theo killed her to keep her from blurting out the truth. Maybe they did let the woman die. Maybe stole some cash or jewelry while they were at it. Maybe Theo wrote the note to make it look like she killed herself," Willie proposed.

Emery crossed one leg over the other. "I don't know, and I'm not going to speculate.

It was quiet for a few minutes, each woman lost in her own thoughts.

Willie broke the silence. "I think we have to consider the possibility that someone wants us to pay for those deaths with our own."

"What?" Emery sat bolt upright. "That's insane."

"She has a point, Doc," Phyl said. "Perhaps our host thinks justice wasn't served and intends to remedy that."

"Then why wasn't Theo killed too?" Emery asked.

Willie shrugged. "Who knows. Theo may be next."

"And the two missing figurines and the poem. The fact that Tamara and Rosie died in the manner laid out in the poem. It's too much of a coincidence," Phyl said.

Emery looked up and shook her head. "You think there's someone on the island besides the eight of us, and that person plans to kill us all?"

Willie and Phyl both nodded.

"That's what I'm thinking," Willie said.

"But Theo swore there was no one else on the island," Emery argued.

"My guess is Theo's either lying, or they will be a victim just like the rest of us."

"I don't think they're lying," Emery said. "Theo's genuinely grieving. And worried and afraid. Just like the rest of us."

Silence filled the void as each woman considered what to do. Phyl looked at Willie and Emery. "I think we all agree that the boat's not coming."

The other two women nodded.

Phyl continued. "And the CB radio has been disabled."

Willie and Emery nodded again.

"So, we've been purposely isolated on this island with no way off and no way to send for help."

"Do you have a plan?" Willie asked.

Phyl slowly raised and lowered her head. "I'm not going to sit around and wait for this psycho to come for me. I say we find him before he kills again."

"I agree," Emery said. "But he's dangerous and crazy as hell."

"Yes, but there's eight of us and only one of him," Phyl reminded them.

"We keep referring to the killer as 'him'. It could be a woman. We really don't have any idea," Willie said.

"You're right," Emery agreed. "A woman could have killed Tamara and Rosie as easily as a man. There's not much strength needed to administer poison."

"I think our next move is to search the house and the island," Phyl said.

"I agree," Emery said. "We should get Darcy to help us. It will be safer in pairs."

"I'm safe enough. I have my gun." Willie patted her side. "I never leave home without it."

"Your what?" Emery said, a confused look on her face.

Willie pulled her jacket to the side, revealing a black snub-nose revolver on her hip. "Ruger 357," she said proudly.

Phyl's eyes opened wide. "You brought a gun to the island? Why?"

Willie pulled her jacket back into place and crossed her arms. "I thought I was coming here in a professional capacity, remember? I'm a private investigator. I have a permit. And all retired cops carry a gun." She shrugged. "Old habits die hard."

Phyl and Emery looked at each other.

"I don't like guns. You having one makes me uncomfortable." Emery looked at Willie. "During my residency, I had to operate on dozens of people with gunshot wounds. The damage they do is devastating."

Willie raised an eyebrow, trying to look nonchalant. "Then let's hope I don't have to shoot anyone." She gave Emery a half-smile.

"Yes, let's hope so." Emery nodded slowly.

The three women headed to the cliff. Darcy still stood near the edge, looking intently out to sea. The wind had increased significantly, causing her long hair to whip around like the snakes on Medusa's head. In the distance, lightning flashed across the sky, and thunderclaps echoed over the water. She didn't turn to greet them as they approached, staring as if in a trance at the approaching storm.

Phyl cleared her throat. "Looks like we're in for a storm."

Darcy turned slowly and glanced at them before turning her attention back to the water. "I'd rather you didn't disturb me. Please leave me alone."

The three looked at each other, confusion written on their faces.

"We wanted to ask you to help us search the island," Emery said.

"I'm not interested. I'd like to be left alone with my thoughts." Her voice was flat and without emotion.

"Are you all right?" Emery asked.

"Yes. I just want to be left alone."

Willie looked at the other two and shrugged. "All right, I guess we'll see you at lunch."

"I'm not hungry," Darcy said, still staring out to sea.

When they were out of hearing distance, Phyl asked, "What's wrong with her? She seemed fine at breakfast."

"I don't know. Maybe the stress is getting to her," Emery said. "I'll try to talk to her privately after lunch."

"I think that's a good idea," Phyl said. "It would be easy for any of us to become paranoid and lose touch with reality."

"You're right. We need to keep a close eye on each other," Willie said.

As they approached the island's west side, all three took out their cell phones and turned them on.

"I've got nothing," Phyl said, holding her phone in the air and moving it around.

"Me either," Emery said.

"Shit," Willie said. "My phone's dead. I forgot to charge it last night. Damn it."

"All right, let's search the rest of the island." Phyl pointed to the darkening clouds moving closer to the island. "That storm will be here soon, and I'd rather not be out here when it hits."

"Agreed," Willie said.

Phyl and Willie walked a dozen or more steps before realizing Emery wasn't with them. They turned back to see Emery looking back at Darcy. "What's wrong, Doc?" Phyl asked.

Emery pulled her attention away and looked at the two women. "I'm concerned about Darcy. Should we have left her? Do you think she's safe out there alone?"

"She's a strong woman, and she's in decent shape. I'm sure she can take care of herself," Willie said.

Emery exhaled. "I suppose you're right." She began walking. "Let's get this over with."

Having found no sign of another living soul on the island except the eight of them, Willie, Phyl, and Emery returned to the house.

"We still have an hour until lunch," Phyl said. "Why don't we split up and search the house and outbuildings?"

"I'll take the garage," Emery said.

"I'll check the first floor and the shed," Willie volunteered.

"I'll take the second and third floors," Phyl said. "Let's meet back here in forty-five minutes.

They split up and began their search. The house was eerily quiet as Phyl proceeded up the stairs to find Theo and ask for the master key to the rooms. She found them on the third floor in their room, holding the hand of their dead wife.

"I'm sorry, Theo. I don't want to disturb you."

Theo looked up, tears in their eyes. "It's okay. I need to get lunch ready anyway."

"Are you sure? We could just throw some sandwiches together ourselves. Everyone would understand."

Theo placed Rosie's hand back under the sheet and stood. "No, I need to stay busy. Sitting here isn't doing anyone any good."

"All right, if you're sure."

"I am." Theo walked to the door and turned to look at Phyl. "She didn't deserve to die."

"No, I'm sure she didn't."

"She had a difficult childhood. Her father was abusive. He killed her mother."

"I guess that explains why she fainted."

"Yes, she hated yelling or loud noises."

"How old was she when her mother died?"

"Six. She was placed in a foster home. She ran away from the last one when she was sixteen. Her foster father tried to rape her."

"The bastard. What did she do after she ran away?"

"She couch-surfed and stayed with friends. She got a cleaning job at a nursing home and started community college when she was seventeen. She wanted to be a nurse."

"Is that where you met her, at college?"

"Yes. She was so smart. She got her Nurses Aid Certificate in two years. She got me a job at the same nursing home." Tears streamed down Theo's face, and they wiped them away. "I don't know what I'll do without her."

Phyl reached out and squeezed their shoulder. "If you need someplace to stay when we leave here, I have some connections in Boston."

"Thanks, that's very nice of you."

Phyl turned to go.

"Ms. Long." Theo stopped her. "What was it you needed?"

"Oh, yes. The key to the rooms. We're searching the house and outbuildings to make sure there's no one hiding. We've already searched the island."

Theo nodded slowly. "I guess that's a good idea." They handed a set of keys to Phyl. "I think some people might be in their rooms. Please knock first."

Phyl chuckled. "That kind of takes away the element of surprise, doesn't it?"

"I suppose so. But I don't think Ms. Ames would take kindly to you barging in on her while she's praying."

"You're right. I wouldn't want to have to deal with her wrath."

Theo stopped at the door. "Do you think anyone would mind if I slept on the couch in the front room tonight? I don't think I can sleep here," they said, looking at Rosie's body on the bed.

"I think it would be fine," Phyl said. "I'll tell everyone at lunch."

After looking in every nook and cranny on the third floor, Phyl made her way down to the second floor. She knocked on each door. When no one answered, she let herself in. Luckily, Catherine wasn't in her room to give her a difficult time. In each room, she looked in the closets, bathrooms, and under the beds. She found nothing amiss. No hidden doors, no trace of anyone or anything that shouldn't be there.

She saved Virgie's room for last. They hadn't had a chance to talk privately and compare notes since their walk that morning. Phyl was eager to hear how her walk with Catherine had gone. She also wanted to spend some time getting to know Virgie better. She knocked softly on the door and waited.

"Who is it?" Virgie asked from the other side.

"It's Phyl. Can I come in?"

She heard the lock turn, and the door opened. Virgie stood there, her eyes red and puffy. Without thinking, Phyl took her in her arms.

"What's wrong?" Phyl asked softly.

Virgie rested her head on Phyl's shoulder. "What isn't? Two people are dead. Someone is accusing the rest of us of horrible things. There's a psycho hiding on the island wanting to do God-knows-what to us." She pulled away and closed the door. "Then there's that judgmental bitch…"

"Catherine?"

Virgie nodded. "She all but admitted that she killed her mother. Or at least caused her mother's death. On her way down to the basement, she tripped over a bag of cat food Catherine deliberately left on one of the steps and broke her neck."

Phyl moved closer to Virgie. "That's horrible."

Tears fell down Virgie's face again. "And that bitch has the nerve to say her mother deserved it. That she had to pay for her sins. She had an affair with a man in their church. Apparently, the punishment for adultery is death." Virgie wiped her face with her sleeve. "And the man her mother had an affair with was killed in a car crash a short time after her mother died."

"Oh my God. Did she kill him too?"

"I don't know, but it's a strange coincidence."

Phyl took her in her arms and gently rubbed her back.

Virgie leaned into Phyl, taking comfort in her embrace. "That woman's twisted the Bible so much it might as well be a pretzel. It's people like her that make me hate religion. It's all fucking bullshit."

Phyl didn't want to argue about it. Her mother had been religious, but she'd been kind and compassionate. She'd never heard an unkind word come out of her mouth.

"Virgie, how is it you know so much about the Bible? How can you cite all those passages off the top of your head?"

Virgie pulled away and walked to the window. Gray-black clouds had rolled in, and rain had begun to fall. She crossed her arms. "My grandfather was an old-school Baptist minister. He preached fire and brimstone every day of the week and twice on Sundays. Fun was not in his vocabulary. His version of the Bible was all about fear and God's retribution. He controlled the congregation with the threat of eternal damnation in the fires of hell."

"That's so different from the church my parents attended."

"Anything he considered frivolous was sinful. Surprisingly, he let me attend Bible camp every summer. That's where I learned to memorize Bible verses. Every summer, there was a contest to see who could recite the most passages. We'd get a piece of candy for each one we could recite." Virgie chuckled and shook her head at the memory. "I wasn't allowed candy at home, so it was a big motivator for me. Every summer, I'd win more candy than any other kid. My last summer there, I recited one hundred Bible verses."

Phyl turned Virgie around and placed her hands around Virgie's waist. "That's a lot of candy for one kid."

"I gave most of it away. It helped me make friends." Virgie smiled and wiped away the tears. "He stopped letting me attend when I turned fourteen. It was a co-ed camp, and he thought boys and girls should be separated to prevent impure thoughts and temptation. Little did he know where my thoughts strayed."

"Already thinking impure thoughts about the other girls?" Phyl walked up behind Virgie and began massaging her shoulders.

Virgie's closed her eyes and let her chin drop to her chest. "That feels really good."

Phyl smiled to herself. "That was my intent."

They were quiet for a few minutes, enjoying the moment.

"Was there any sign of the boat?" Virgie raised her head.

Phyl stepped away and looked out the window. "No. We've come to the conclusion that it's not coming."

"We?"

"Dr. Brennan, Willie, and I. We decided to search the island and the house to find whoever is behind this."

"And?"

She turned back to Virgie. "No trace of anyone other than the ten of us. Well, the eight of us now." Phyl frowned. "And we didn't find any caves or places someone could hide. Emery's searching the garage and Willie the shed. I hope they have better luck than I did."

"Do you think someone else is hiding on the island?"

Phyl reached out and softly touched Virgie's cheek with the back of her hand. "I hope so."

Virgie leaned into Phyl's touch. She pulled back when the words registered. "What? Why?"

Phyl took a deep breath and let it out, still caressing Virgie's cheek. "Because if there isn't, that means one of us is a killer."

Virgie reached up and covered Phyl's hand with her own. "Oh shit, you're right."

Phyl nodded. Not breaking their gaze, she bent down and placed her lips on Virgie's.

A half-hour later, Phyl walked down the stairs into the dining room. Emery, Willie, and Joan were already there. Their conversation looked heated.

"What's going on? Did you find something?" Phyl asked.

Virgie walked up behind her. "Is something wrong?"

Emery turned her attention away from Joan and said, "We didn't find anything. No sign of another person hiding anywhere."

"What the hell are you three up to? Why all this commotion and suspicious behavior?" Joan demanded as she pulled a cigarette and lighter from her jacket pocket.

"You can't smoke that in here. You can get away with it outside, but not in the house." Virgie stared daggers at the older woman.

"Says who?" Joan raised her chin.

"Me." Virgie glared at her. "I don't care who you used to be. Stop being an arrogant asshole who thinks rules don't apply to them." Virgie's eyes narrowed. "If you want to smoke, go outside. I know it's difficult for you but try to think about other people for a change."

Joan stared at Virgie, the cigarette halfway to her mouth. She smirked and returned the cigarette and lighter to her pocket. "I guess you told me, didn't you?" Joan chuckled. "I like people who aren't afraid of me, who stand up for themselves."

Virgie's shoulders visibly relaxed. She turned to Phyl and smiled.

Phyl returned the smile, then turned to Willie. "So, nothing? There's no one else on the island?"

Willie shook her head. "No, just the ten…I mean, just the eight of us."

"Shit," Virgie said.

"What the hell is going on? What is all this about?" Joan demanded.

Phyl turned to her. "Let's get everyone to the table, and we can all talk about it."

"Theo and Catherine are in the kitchen. I'll get them," Emery said.

"I think Darcy is still out by the cliff," Willie said.

"I'll go get her," Virgie volunteered.

Phyl nodded.

A woman screamed from somewhere outside the house.

"That was Virgie," Phyl said as she ran for the front door. Outside, she could barely see Virgie off in the distance on her hands and knees, looking over the edge of the cliff. Phyl, followed by Willie, Emery, and Theo, took off running, and Joan trailed behind. Phyl arrived first and knelt next to Virgie.

"What is it? What's wrong?"

Virgie looked at her, fear in her eyes. "It's Darcy. She's down there." She pointed to the ocean thirty feet below.

Phyl looked over the edge. Floating in the tide was Darcy, face down and not moving.

Willie, Emery, and Theo fell in beside them. "What is it?" Willie asked, gasping for breath.

"Not what," Phyl said. "Who."

"What do you mean? Is someone down there? Is it Frankie with the boat?" Emery dropped to her knees and crawled to the edge to look.

"No, it's not Frankie. It's Darcy," Virgie said. "I think she's dead."

"What happened? Did she fall?" Willie asked, her face red from exertion. She stood and glared at Virgie. "Or did you push her?"

All eyes zeroed in on Willie, then turned to Virgie, who jumped up, her hands clenched into fists.

"What? Are you crazy? She must have fallen," Virgie yelled.

"Maybe, maybe not," Willie shot back.

Phyl stepped in between the two. "That's enough, Willie."

"Of course, you would take her side." Willie pointed at Virgie. "The two of you are thick as thieves."

Phyl took a step toward Willie. "What exactly—"

"Stop it," Joan demanded. "This isn't helping matters."

"You're right." Phyl rubbed her hands on her thighs. "Theo, can you help me carry Darcy up?"

"Of course, Ms. Long."

"Three people are dead, Theo. I think we can do away with formalities. Call me Phyl."

Theo nodded. "Okay, Phyl. Let's go get her."

The two headed for the stairs down to the dock. Darcy's body had landed in the water nearby. The tide had just begun to come in, and the water was only waist-deep. A tiny stretch of beach appeared when the tide was fully out, and only a flat-bottom skiff could make it to the dock.

Phyl stepped onto the dock first, Theo right behind her. "I'll bring her in. Can you pull her onto the dock?" Phyl asked.

"I think so. She didn't look like she weighed more than one-twenty."

"Between the two of us, we should be able to get her up the stairs," Phyl said, jumping into the ice-blue water. "FUCK! It's cold."

Holding her arms out of the icy water to keep her hands from going numb, she made her way over to the body, the tide pushing her toward the cliff wall when it rushed in. *It's better than the tide going out and dragging us out with it.*

Grabbing one of Darcy's arms, she turned the body over. Darcy's lips were blue. She was obviously dead, but to be sure, Phyl put two fingers against the vein in Darcy's neck. She didn't feel a pulse. She grabbed the body by the arm and tugged it back to the dock, one small step at a time, her legs growing numb in the cold water.

Phyl pushed the body the final distance. Theo bent down, put their hands under Darcy's armpits, and pulled the lifeless body onto the dock, then reached down to help Phyl out of the water.

"It's not going to be easy carrying her up those stairs," Theo said. "She's literally deadweight."

"Give me a minute to catch my breath. We'll figure it out," Phyl said, reaching out. Theo grabbed her hand and hauled her to her feet. "I have an idea. You take her feet and hold them under one arm if you can so you can still walk facing forward. I'll grab under her armpits."

"Okay. We can stop halfway up and switch if you get tired."

"It's only forty steps. I think we can make it."

Theo took off their jacket, tied it tightly around Darcy's legs to keep them together, and tucked them under their arm close to their body. Phyl squatted, slid one hand under each armpit, and locked her hands across Darcy's chest.

Phyl took a deep breath. "All right, let's go."

Theo nodded. The two began the slow climb up the stairs. Phyl's feet and legs were numb from the cold. She slipped once but managed not to drop the body. When they reached the top of the stairs, Willie and Emery relieved them of the body and laid it on the ground.

While Theo and Phyl were bringing Darcy's body up, Catherine and Joan had made their way out to the cliff.

"Another suicide," Catherine said flatly.

"No." Joan shook her head. "That would be too much of a coincidence."

"What do you mean? What else could it be?" Catherine shrieked.

"Let's get back to the house. The weather's getting worse, and Phyl and Theo need to get out of those wet clothes," Emery said.

"Phyl, Theo, you two should go ahead. Change clothes and get warm," Virgie said. "I'll get a blanket to wrap her body. That will make it easier to carry her to the house."

Phyl nodded. "Thanks, Virgie. Theo, let's get out of these clothes and get a drink. I'd say we both deserve one."

"No argument from me," Theo said, walking quickly to the house.

Virgie put her arm around Phyl's waist as they walked up the lawn to the house. "She could've slipped."

"I don't think it was an accident," Phyl said, looking straight ahead.

Virgie stopped walking. "You don't think I did it, do you?"

Phyl stopped, turned to Virgie and searched her eyes. "Honestly, I don't know what to believe anymore." She cupped Virgie's cheek with her hand. "But no, I don't think you killed her."

CHAPTER EIGHT

Saturday Afternoon

The rain began to fall as Willie and Emery carried Darcy's body into the house and up the stairs.

"I need a drink," Willie groaned as they placed the body on the bed Darcy had occupied the night before.

"You go ahead. I'm going to have a look at the body," Emery said as she pulled the blanket away, exposing Darcy's now bluish-purple face and her wide-open eyes. Emery reached down and closed them.

"Okay, I'll leave you to it," Willie said as she hurried out of the room.

In their own rooms, Phyl and Theo took hot showers and changed their clothes while Virgie and Catherine silently made sandwiches for the group. Joan sat alone on the terrace under an eve, sheltered from the rain, smoking.

An hour later, the seven reassembled in the dining room.

"What the hell is going on?" Willie slammed her hand on the table, and everyone jumped. She glared at Virgie. "You—"

"I think they were murdered," Phyl spoke over Willie and pointed to the little castaways on the shelf. Only seven remained.

Catherine looked at the shelf and back to Phyl. "Don't be ridiculous. They could have been accidents. Darcy could have stumbled and fallen."

Emery pursed her lips and shook her head. "Darcy's death wasn't suicide or an accident. She was murdered."

"No," Virgie cried out. "No, no, no."

Phyl looked at Virgie and then turned to Emery. "Are you sure?"

"Positive. There's a gash in the back of her head, about the size of a quarter. If I had to guess, I'd say the murder weapon was a hammer." Emery paused to look at each person in the room. "Someone snuck up behind her and hit her with it. The force of the blow would have been enough to send her over the cliff."

Willie pounded her fist on the table, then pointed at Emery. "You could have done it. You searched the garage. You got the hammer there, didn't you?"

Emery's head jerked up, her eyebrows arched, then lowered. "And you searched the shed. It's just as likely that there was a hammer in there."

Willie's face turned crimson, and she took a step toward Emery only to be restrained by Theo.

"Let go of me!" Willie yelled, fighting to pull away, but Theo held tight to Willie's arm.

"That's enough, Willie!" Joan shouted.

Willie refocused her anger on Joan. "Fuck you!" she yelled, a tiny bit of spittle flying from her mouth. She narrowed her eyes and glared at Joan. "You aren't in charge; you don't get to tell me what to do."

"Please, Willie, calm down," Phyl said. "Why don't we all take a deep breath." She looked at Willie, then the others.

"Yes, let's all have a seat and calm down," Joan agreed.

Phyl grabbed the back of a chair and pulled it out. No one else made a move to comply. Willie glared at Joan, then at Emery, then back at Joan.

Calmly, Virgie pulled out a chair and sat. "Please, everyone, take a seat."

Catherine and Emery pulled chairs out and sat. Theo looked at Joan, who nodded to release Willie's arm. They pulled out a chair next to Willie. "Willie," they said, "please sit down."

Willie took a long breath and forced her shoulders back. "Fine." She sat, crossing her arms like a petulant child.

When they were all seated, Joan turned to Emery. "What about Tamara and Rosie?"

"I don't think they killed themselves, at least not Tamara. I've looked through her possessions and the clothing she was wearing. There's no container or baggie for the poison." She looked at each person around the table. "If she had brought it to the island intending to kill herself, how did she get it here? It would have had to be in something, and there's nothing like that on her body or possessions." She paused to think. "If we were talking only about Rosie or Darcy, my first guess would've been an accidental death. Maybe Rosie took something, and it killed her?" She looked at Theo and grimaced, then turned her attention back to the others. "But we haven't found any kind of substance, legal or otherwise, in her room that would be suspect." Emery laced her fingers together on the table and blew out a breath. "And the whites of her eyes were red. That suggests suffocation."

Virgie gasped. "What?"

Willie turned on Theo. "You suffocated her?"

Theo's eyes bulged, and their mouth fell open. "No. No, I could never hurt Rosie. I love—" They choked back a sob as they looked around the table. "I loved her."

"But you were the last one with her," Willie insisted.

Theo shook their head. "I didn't want to wake her, so I slept in the front room." They took a breath. "Any one of you could have snuck into our room after I went back downstairs."

"Did anyone see you downstairs?" Joan asked.

Theo shook their head.

Willie glared at them. "You killed her, didn't you?"

Shocked, no one said anything for several seconds.

"All right, three people are dead in less than twenty-four hours," Joan said. "And there's the missing figurine every time someone dies. That's not a coincidence."

"You're an amateur botanist," Virgie said, staring at Emery.

Emery cocked her head to the side. "Yes. So what?"

"So, you could have made the poison that killed Tamara."

"I know a lot about trees and plants, but I'm not a chemist," Emery argued.

"But you know which ones are deadly."

Emery's face grew heated. "Anyone can look that up on the Internet."

Willie glared across the table at Emery. "What did you give Rosie last night to help her sleep?"

Emery stared back at the woman. "Nothing. When I checked on her, she was asleep. I took her vital signs and left."

"So you say. Maybe you smothered her." Willie glowered.

Emery stood and leaned on the table with both hands. "Are you accusing me of murder?"

"Maybe. How much did you drink last night?"

"I don't drink," Emery said, her hands clenched into fists.

Willie cocked her head slightly to the side. "Why? Do you have a problem with alcohol?"

"Damn it, Willie, I don't know where you're going with this. I don't drink because I need to keep my wits about me. You never know when someone will have a medical emergency."

Phyl raised her hands in the air. "Stop it! That's enough. We need to keep our heads on straight." She looked at Emery. "Please, Emery. Sit back down."

The doctor glared at Willie for a second before taking her seat.

Willie shrugged. "I was only raising the possibility."

"First off, I didn't give Rosie anything last night. And second, she was alive when Theo checked on her later."

Willie wasn't ready to give in. "Maybe she was, maybe she wasn't."

"That's enough, Willie!" Phyl shouted.

From the other side of the room, Catherine said, "John 8:7. 'Let he who is without sin cast the first stone.'"

Willie turned on her. "What the hell is that supposed to mean?"

Catherine sat, her back perfectly straight, not backing down. "You committed perjury and caused a boy's death. You have no right to judge the doctor."

Virgie leaned over and whispered into Phyl's ear, "Talk about the kettle calling the pot black. She takes the cake." Phyl nodded but didn't say anything.

"To hell with all of you," Willie raged. "I did what needed to be done to get a thug off the streets. Everyone wants the police to keep them safe, and then they complain about how it gets done."

Emery looked across the table at Willie and smirked. "I think you all have a right to know that Willie brought a gun to the island."

There were several audible gasps. "What the hell for?" Joan asked.

"I'm a retired cop. We all carry guns. And I have a permit."

"That doesn't make me feel any safer," Virgie said.

"Look, I was supposedly hired to provide security. I know now that was a lie. But at the time, I thought it best to bring it." She folded her arms defensively. "Good thing I did, considering three people are dead."

After lunch, they met in the front room except Theo, who remained in the kitchen cleaning up and preparing a pot of tea. Joan, Willie, and Phyl drank scotch while Virgie drank wine. Emery and Catherine waited for tea.

Joan stood in front of the fireplace, warming herself. Outside, the wind and rain pounded against the sides of the house, making it creak and groan like a worn-out machine. The windows rattled in their frames, letting in gusts of cold air. Once or twice, the lights flickered when a gust of wind rocked the house.

Virgie sat in a wingback chair in front of the fire. "I hope to God the electricity doesn't go out. That's the last thing we need."

"You pray to God," Catherine corrected her as she took out her knitting needles and yarn from a bag at her feet. "You don't hope to God."

"Don't get your panties in a twist. It's just a saying. And I don't pray. It's a waste of time," Virgie added just to piss off Catherine.

Catherine, however, didn't take the bait. Instead, she clicked her tongue several times and shook her head.

Theo entered the room, placed a tray with a pot of tea and two cups on the coffee table, then turned to leave.

Phyl stopped them. "Theo, have a seat."

Theo looked around. "Are you sure?"

Phyl nodded. "There's seven figurines. There's seven of us. You're one of the castaways."

Everyone agreed, and Theo sat on the sofa—right where Tamara sat before she died.

Joan turned from the fire and looked at Emery. "Is there any chance the gash on the back of Darcy's head happened in the fall? Maybe her head hit a rock?"

Emery breathed out a sigh. "No."

"Why not?" Joan pressed, her judge demeanor in full gear.

"The gash was a perfect circle. About an inch and a half across," she said. "If she'd hit a rock, the gash would be jagged and irregular."

"So, not an accident and not suicide," Joan said.

"No, it wasn't an accident, and Darcy didn't kill herself. Not even a contortionist could hit herself on the back of the head with that kind of force."

Joan took a long drink from her glass and looked at each person in the room. "So, the person who lured us to the island intends to kill us all."

"I believe so," Emery said.

"The three of you searched the island and house earlier this morning." Joan looked at Phyl. "And you didn't find anyone else?"

Phyl shook her head. "No. There's no one else on the island."

"How is that possible?" Virgie asked.

"I'll tell you how," Joan said. "Because the only explanation is the killer is in this room."

"No," Virgie said as she lowered her head into her hands. "God, no."

Catherine laughed out loud, and all eyes looked at her questioningly. "I find it amusing that Virginia doesn't believe in God, yet she continually calls on him for help." She shook her head. "It's quite funny, don't you think?"

"There's nothing funny about anything going on here," Phyl said.

Joan agreed, "We're all in danger. Someone in this room brought us all here to kill us. One of you has appointed yourself judge, jury, and executioner to right some perceived wrong they think we've each committed."

Seven sets of eyes looked from one to another.

Joan continued, "Of the ten people who came to this island, three are dead. So obviously, we can rule them out." She paused. "Ladies and Theo, one of us is a fake little castaway."

Catherine continued to knit; the others seemed to be at a loss for words. Without looking up from her knitting, Catherine said, "I agree with the judge. One of us is possessed by the devil."

Virgie took a large gulp of wine. "Jesus, give it a rest."

Catherine made a tsking noise with her tongue again. "So, now you're bringing the Lord's son into it?"

"I may kill her myself," Virgie said, emptying her glass.

"Virgie, that's not funny," Emery said.

Virgie shrugged as she stood and went to the bar.

"We have to figure out which one of us it is," Phyl said.

"Agreed," Joan said.

Emery sat up straight. "I'm a doctor. I took an oath to do no harm."

"Plenty of doctors have killed innocent babies," Catherine pointed out.

Emery frowned but didn't argue the point.

Joan cleared her throat. "I was a judge for over twenty years. I swore to uphold the law."

"What about the judge who went to prison for taking huge payoffs to send kids to private for-profit treatment facilities," Virgie asked, a single eyebrow raised.

Joan, red-faced, stared at her without saying a word.

"I was a cop; I'm—"

"Don't go there, Willie," Emery warned. "Every time you turn on the news, a cop's been arrested for some crime or another."

Catherine continued knitting; without looking up, she said, "You all know I'm a Christian woman. I would never harm a soul."

Virgie and Theo looked at each other. It was all they could do not to laugh.

"Catherine, you're about as Christian as my ass," Virgie said.

Catherine looked up from her knitting and pointed the long metal needles at Virgie and Theo. "Heathens," she muttered.

"I thought I took those away from you," Emery said.

Catherine smiled smugly. "I have several pairs." She returned to her knitting.

Willie crossed an ankle over her knee. "You know poison is the weapon of choice among older women who kill."

"True. Even so-called Christian women have used poison to kill. Although they usually target men," Joan added.

Theo raised their hand. "I should be ruled out. I loved my wife."

Joan and Willie shook their heads and looked at each other. "After you, Judge," Willie demurred.

"Thank you, Willie." Joan nodded and crossed her arms. "Domestic violence is at epidemic proportions in this country. And not just in the heterosexual population. There're no boundaries when it comes to killing one's spouse."

"Maybe we should determine who has alibis at the time of each death," Emery said. "That should eliminate some of us."

"Good idea," Phyl said. "I'll point out that Theo wasn't in the room when Tamara died, and they and Catherine were together when Darcy was killed."

Everyone nodded in agreement.

"As for Rosie's death," Joan said, "the doctor and Theo were both alone with her. But if Theo is telling the truth about sleeping downstairs, someone could have killed her after Theo left."

"I saw Willie leave the room just before Tamara died last night. She could've been getting the poison," Virgie said with a raised eyebrow.

"I went to use the restroom," Willie sneered. "And I saw Virgie leave the room right after I came back."

"Yes, I went to the restroom also," Virgie said. "But I was only gone a minute."

"Well, forgive me for having to do more than pee," Willie said defensively.

"I used the restroom also," Catherine volunteered. "But it's ridiculous to think that I could harm anyone."

Virgie leaned over to Theo and whispered, "She's at the top of my list." Theo gave her an almost imperceptible nod of agreement.

"So, who was the last one to see Darcy alive?" Joan asked.

"I talked to her after I left Catherine on the west side of the island," Virgie said.

"Catherine, did you see Darcy?" Joan asked.

"No. I walked around the other side of the island and came in through the back of the house."

"The three of us talked to her when we searched the island." Phyl pointed to herself, Willie, and Emery. "That was after Virgie talked to her. She was still out there when we got back."

"Virgie, after you returned, where did you go? Can anyone confirm your whereabouts just before lunch?" asked Joan.

"Yes, I spoke briefly to Phyl on the terrace before I went to my room to lie down. Phyl came by a little later to check on me."

Joan turned to face Catherine. "What about you, Catherine?"

"I was in the kitchen helping Theo prepare lunch."

"Theo, can you confirm that?" Joan asked.

"She was there when I came down with my blanket and pillow." Theo looked at the others. "I'm going to sleep down here again if no one minds." No one did.

"Phyl, what did you do after you returned from searching the island?" Joan questioned.

"First, I searched the third floor. That's where I ran into Theo. I told them I didn't think anyone would mind if they slept down here."

"I agree. It wouldn't be right to make them sleep in the same room with their dead wife," Virgie said.

Phyl nodded. "Then I went to the second floor and searched all the guest rooms."

"You went into our rooms?" Catherine's voice rose. "What right did you have to invade our privacy?"

"Need I remind you that there's a killer on the loose? Time was of the essence," Phyl said.

"Still, I think you could have waited and gotten our permission," Catherine said.

"If I had, whoever is the killer could've disposed of the evidence," Phyl reminded her.

Joan cut in, "Phyl, can anyone corroborate your story?"

"I checked Virgie's room last. We talked for a while before coming down together."

Joan turned to Willie. "Where did you go after the three of you returned?"

"I searched the first floor and the shed behind the house."

"Did anyone see you?"

"No, I didn't see a soul. And I didn't go out front, so I don't know if Darcy was still out there."

"Doctor, what about you?" Joan asked.

"I went to the garage and searched it. I didn't see anyone, and I came in the back door, so I didn't see Darcy either."

"Did anyone see you during that time?"

"Not until I came in through the back door. Theo and Catherine were in the kitchen."

"Well, that just leaves me," Joan said. "I was out on the terrace since that's the only place I can smoke—"

"You're not supposed to smoke anywhere on the island," Virgie reminded her.

"Stop blathering about my smoking. The killer isn't playing by any rules. I see no reason why I should."

Virgie chuckled. "Did you say blathering?"

Joan stared at her, her eyes laser focused. How dare she insult her, make fun of her. The woman was a nobody. Joan was destined to be a United States congresswoman. She'd given her a pass once, not again. "Being a teacher, I would have thought you'd have a greater appreciation for a robust vocabulary. I see now that I was wrong about you. You, like most people your age, choose to use the most common of words to express yourself."

Virgie laughed outright this time. "Joan, you're nothing but a pompous ass and a blowhard with a superiority complex."

Willie snickered. "I'd say she expressed herself very well that time, Joan. Pompous ass, blowhard, superiority complex. They all beat blathering, hands down."

Joan clenched and unclenched her fists, then took a deep breath and slowly let it out. She forced herself to regain some sense of professionalism. Returning the cigarette and lighter to her pocket, she turned back to the group. "As I was saying, Phyl, Willie, and the doctor saw me when they headed out on their mission. Before their return, I moved into this room to escape the wind. Darcy was still standing out there. I was alone until Willie and Emery came in just before lunch."

"So, Theo is the only one we can rule out as the killer based on their absence when Tamara died," Virgie added.

"Yes," Joan said. "Virgie, you were alone from the time you entered the house until Phyl knocked on your door."

Virgie nodded.

Joan continued, "Phyl, you were alone for a short time after you talked to Theo until you entered Virgie's room."

"Yes, that's correct," Phyl said. "No more than ten minutes. Not enough time to run out to the cliff and back."

"Willie, you were alone from the time you left Emery and Phyl until you reentered the house after searching the shed."

"That's correct," Willie said.

"Doctor, you were alone from the same time until you returned from searching the garage, correct?"

"Yes." Emery nodded.

Joan turned to Catherine next. "Ms. Ames, you were alone from the time you and Virgie parted ways until you entered the kitchen to help Theo."

"Yes, that is correct," Catherine said.

"And I was alone from the time those three left the terrace until we all met in the dining room." Joan took a step closer to the window. The only sound came from the storm outside and the crackle of burning wood in the fireplace.

"So, I can be ruled out," Phyl said. "I never left the room before Tamara died, and ten minutes wouldn't have been enough time to run out to the cliff, push Darcy off, and run back upstairs."

"And you weren't winded when you got to my room," Virgie offered.

"However, Emery, Willie, Virgie, Catherine, and I cannot be ruled out," Joan said. "Each of us were alone for a while just before Darcy's body was found."

Virgie began to cry. "I can't believe you could think I killed those people."

"That's not what I'm saying. We're just looking at the facts," Joan said.

"You were also the one who went out to the cliff to get Darcy," Willie said. "You could have pushed her."

"That's crazy," Virgie shouted.

"All right, that's enough," Joan said, refocusing everyone's attention on her. "We have five people who we cannot eliminate from suspicion."

"I agree," Phyl said. "For now, though, all we can do is keep trying to reach the authorities. That means taking turns walking to the west side of the island whenever there's a break in the storm. I suggest we do that in groups of three. No one goes anywhere alone."

"Yes, we each need to be aware of our surroundings and keep our guard up. Don't take any unnecessary risks," Joan said.

Virgie wrapped her arms around her waist. "I can't believe this is happening."

"I think six of us would agree with you," Joan said. "The seventh is probably taking great delight in our fear."

CHAPTER NINE

"You're not having second thoughts are you? About me killing them?" Virgie asked.

She and Phyl were in her room, seated in front of the window, watching the storm. The wind screamed like a banshee outside. The rain sounded like handfuls of stones being repeatedly flung against the house.

Phyl paused before answering. How well did she actually know this woman? Truth be told, not very well. *I want to believe her, but how can I be sure?* She turned her head to look at her. "No, I don't." She took Virgie's hand. "I'm staking my life on it."

Virgie let out the breath she'd been holding and took Phyl's hand. "Thank you."

"But I agree with Joan. One of them is dangerous."

"It's a nightmare. I can't wrap my head around the fact that three people are dead—"

"And the killer isn't done yet."

Virgie sighed. "It's bizarre. I wasn't really worried until Darcy's death. I really believed Tamara's and Rosie's deaths could have been suicides or accidents. But Darcy was definitely murdered. So, it's probable that the other two were as well."

"Yes," Phyl agreed. "And there's the little figurines. Three are gone, and I sure as hell don't think they marched away on their own."

"No. The killer took each one when no one was looking."

Phyl ran a hand through her hair. "Whoever is doing this planned it out, every last detail."

"What kind of sicko does this?"

"Someone with a god complex who thinks they have the right to punish others," Phyl said.

Virgie stared at her. "Catherine? She admits to killing her mother and her mother's lover."

"She is the most obvious suspect." Phyl slowly rubbed her thumb across the back of Virgie's hand. "But the killer could have brought her here to be a decoy. To divert suspicion."

"Then who do you think it is?" Virgie asked.

Phyl took a deep breath and let it out. "Emery. No one has brought up the fact that she gave Tamara a glass of water shortly before she collapsed. Maybe the poison was in it? She knows a lot about plants, so like you said, she could have made a poison." Phyl paused. "And she did go into Rosie's room by herself, and no one really knows how long she was there. She could have given her something, and Rosie wouldn't have questioned it. Hell, she could've injected her with something."

Virgie sucked in a breath. "Oh my God, you're right. She probably has all kinds of drugs in her bag. And I'd forgotten about the glass of water. We were all focused on the scotch."

"And she was by herself in the garage. She could've found a hammer, snuck out to the cliff, and killed Darcy."

Virgie looked out the window, considering this information. "I hadn't really thought about that." She looked back at Phyl. "She doesn't look like a killer, though."

"Neither did Lizzy Borden and look how that turned out for her parents."

"Theo, who do you think killed them?" Willie asked as Theo deposited blankets and a pillow on the sofa. Across the room, Joan and Emery stood looking out the windows at the storm.

"If you're asking if I think it's you, I don't."

"Well, thanks for that." Willie patted them on the shoulder. "But you must be suspicious of someone."

"I don't think it's Virgie. She's just too nice to be a killer, don't you think?"

Willie shrugged. "I've known some sociopaths who could charm the skin off a snake one minute and stab you in the gut the next."

Theo stared at her. "That's not very reassuring."

"Sorry, but it's true. People who are nice to your face aren't always what they seem."

"This whole thing's a nightmare." Theo stuffed a pillow into a pillowcase. "We've been here a little more than a day, and three people, including my wife, have been murdered."

"And worse, it's probably not the end of it." Willie raised a single eyebrow and then excused herself to retire to her room.

Joan stared out the window in the front room, wishing she could have a cigarette. Her nerves were shot. Unfortunately, the storm hadn't let up, and going outside was out of the question.

Emery stood, shoved her hands in her pockets, and paced from one side of the room to the other. "We have to get off this island," she said to no one in particular.

"By the looks of the storm, we aren't going anywhere for a while," Joan said without turning away from the window. "Anyone who'd come out here in this weather would have to have a death wish."

Emery collapsed back onto the chair next to Joan and dropped her head into her hands. "Staying here any longer could mean the death of us all." She looked up. "All but one of us anyway."

"I hope not," Joan said.

"Three people are dead. It doesn't bode well for the rest of us."

Joan turned from the window and looked at Emery. "Those three were caught off guard. They weren't expecting it. We know now that we're being hunted. We need to take precautions."

"Hunted?"

Joan frowned. "Isn't that what she's doing? Hunting us like we're prey?"

"You don't suspect me, do you?"

"To be honest with you, Doctor, I haven't ruled anyone out," Joan said. "I don't issue rulings until all the evidence is in. Pieces of the puzzle are still missing."

"Like what?"

Joan smiled. "Ah, no, you don't. I'm not sharing my concerns with you. What if you're the killer? That would help you stalk us, wouldn't it?"

"You make a good point, Judge." Emery slowly nodded. "You do make a good point."

Catherine perched on the edge of her bed and silently read her Bible.

...and if the witness is a false witness and has accused his brother falsely, then you shall do to him as he had meant to do to his brother. So, you shall purge the evil from your midst. And the rest shall hear and fear and shall never again commit any such evil among you. Your eye shall not pity. It shall be life for life, eye for an eye, tooth for tooth, hand for hand, foot for foot.

She closed the Bible, placed it beside her, climbed off the bed, and knelt. She held her hands together in prayer. *Dear Lord. Thy will be done.*

Dinner had been a quiet affair. Joan claimed she loved to cook and volunteered to make spaghetti, surprising everyone. Virgie made a salad, and Phyl sliced a loaf of French bread, spread garlic butter on it, and tossed it into the oven.

At the table, eyes darted from one to another. Six of the seven worried about who the killer was and who would be their next victim. The seventh, a master of deception, looked just as concerned as the others.

Afterward, in the front room, everyone kept to themselves. Outside, the storm raged on. Gale-force winds and rain continued their attack on the house. Occasionally, lightning flashed across the sky, and thunder caused the windowpanes to rattle.

Theo knelt in front of the fireplace, adding more logs to the fire. "I'll chop more wood in the morning. We've gone through all that I chopped before everyone arrived. It's hard to believe that was just yester—" Their voice cracked. "I'm sorry. It's just so hard to believe Rosie's dead." A tear ran down their face. "How could someone…one of you, kill her? WHY?" Theo demanded, throwing down the poker.

Virgie went to Theo and placed a hand on their shoulder. "I'm so sorry, Theo. I wish none of us had ever come here."

Catherine sat in the wingback chair and briefly looked up from her knitting. "It is not our place to question God's plan. He brought us here for a reason. Those that believe in him will be protected."

Virgie, her fingers clenched into fists, wheeled around to face her. "I swear to fucking God I will shove one of those needles up your ass if you say another word!" Except for the noise from the storm and the crackling of the fire, the room was silent. Catherine's face went white. Her mouth hung open, and her eyes grew to the size of silver dollars.

Phyl stepped in front of Virgie and placed both hands on her shoulders. "Stop. I know you're upset and afraid. We all are. But that doesn't help." She moved a hand to Virgie's cheek. "Close your eyes, take a deep breath."

Virgie closed her eyes, breathed in, and exhaled slowly. "I'm okay. I just can't stand that woman."

Catherine stood and scowled at Virgie. "You're okay? What about me? That's the second time you've threatened to kill me. You're the one we should all be afraid of. I certainly am."

"Give me a break. You're the crazy one here. You and all your religious bullshit."

Catherine shoved her knitting needles and yarn into her bag. "I will not sit here and be insulted by a heathen like you. I'm going to my room and locking the door."

Virgie crossed her arms. "Good."

"Good night, Catherine," Joan said. "Try to get a good night's rest."

The others murmured good night as Catherine left the room.

Phyl led Virgie to the sofa and motioned for her to sit. "You can't let her get to you like that." Phyl dropped down beside her. "She's a bitch, but you going off like that just makes it worse."

"Phyl's right," Emery said. "We're all at our wit's end. Attacking each other only helps the killer."

"You're right. She just says such horribly inappropriate things." Virgie placed her hand on Phyl's knee.

Willie looked at Emery, jerked her head toward the couple, and raised an eyebrow. Emery shrugged and then cleared her throat. "I hate to have to bring this up, and, Theo, I'm very sorry you have to hear this." She looked at Theo, then the others. "But the bodies are going to start putting out a very unpleasant odor tomorrow. We'll need to keep wet towels at the bottom of each door to try to keep the smell contained inside the rooms."

Willie pointed to the bowl of red-and-white peppermint candies on the bar. "When I was a cop, I carried those with me. Sucking on them helps."

"And so will anything with a strong menthol or eucalyptus scent, like Vick's Vapor Rub," Emery said. "You can dab it under your nose if you have to go into one of the rooms."

"I have a jar of Vick's in my bag. I brought in case one of the children came down with a cold," Virgie said. "The nonexistent children."

"Good," said Emery. "We should keep those doors closed unless it's absolutely necessary to open them."

No one knew what to say about what was to come. The only sound in the room was Theo, who had begun to cry again.

Finally, Joan spoke up. "Would anyone like a nightcap? I could use a small one to help me sleep."

Theo stood. "I'll get it for you. Dr. Brennan, can I make you a cup of tea?" they asked, wiping the tears from their face with the sleeve of their shirt.

"Thanks, Theo, but I think I'll head off to my room." Emery stood. "Good night."

"Good night," the others replied.

Theo walked behind the bar. "Does anyone else want something?"

"Scotch for me," Willie said.

"Phyl, Virgie, anything for you?" they asked.

"Scotch for me also," Phyl said.

"I'll have a glass of merlot," Virgie said, then paused. "Theo?"

They looked up from pouring scotch into three glasses. "Yes?"

"Would you mind opening a new bottle? Just to be safe?"

Theo nodded. "Of course."

Virgie looked at the others. "It doesn't hurt to be safe, right?"

The four nodded in agreement.

After Theo handed out the glasses of scotch and a glass of wine to Virgie, they reached for a bottle of tequila and poured the clear liquid into a shot glass.

Joan raised her glass. "Here's to getting off this fucking island tomorrow."

"Here's to getting off this island alive," Willie corrected.

"I'll drink to that," Phyl said.

CHAPTER TEN

Early Sunday Morning

Sweat trickled down Theo's back as they raised an ax over their head for what seemed like the hundredth time that morning. It felt good to be outside in the fresh air. Doing something physical helped take their mind off Rosie, at least for a little while. They swiftly brought the ax down, splitting the log in two with a thunk. As they bent over, picked up the pieces, and tossed them onto the growing pile of firewood, thoughts of Rosie filled their head. Could it have been only two days ago that they'd taken a walk around the island, snapping pictures of themselves, smiling? A sob rose in their throat, and they swallowed hard to force it back down. They didn't have time to grieve right now; they needed to get the logs split and the wood in the house before the sky opened and let loose more rain. Luckily, the previous night's storm hadn't blown the tarp off the woodpile, and the logs were dry, but it wouldn't be long before the storm returned. The wind had picked up, pushing trees almost to their breaking point. Occasionally, there was a loud crack, then the crash of a branch hitting the ground. They hurried to split another dozen logs as thunder roared in the distance.

As they raised the ax over their head again, something cracked behind them. They stopped midswing, lowered the ax, and turned around.

Their eyes grew wide. "You…"

Before Theo could utter another word, the killer's ax cut through their raised arm, nearly severing it. The second swing plunged into their forehead with a thunk, echoing the sound of an ax splitting a log in two.

Phyl had always been an early riser, always awake as soon as the sun broke over the horizon. This morning was no different. What was different was that she wasn't alone.

When they'd all gone upstairs last night, Phyl walked Virgie to her room.

"Want to come in and talk?" Virgie had asked when they reached the door.

"Sure, just for a little while. I want to be up early to go to the other side of the island and try to get cell reception on my phone."

Laying on the bed, fully clothed, they talked about anything other than death. That had led to kissing, which led to the shedding of clothes and Phyl waking up naked in Virgie's bed the next morning.

She leaned on an elbow and looked at the still-sleeping woman beside her. *I hope to God you aren't the killer.*

She turned over and looked out the window. The storm had calmed some, but the wind was still furious, blowing around anything not battened down and rustling tree branches mercilessly. She nudged Virgie. "Hey, it's time to wake up."

Virgie rolled over, opened one eye, and smiled. "I guess last night wasn't a dream."

"No, it wasn't." Phyl climbed out of the bed. "But we need to get dressed and go see if we can get cell reception. The rain's stopped, so let's get going before it starts again."

"No shower?" Virgie pouted.

"As soon as we're off this island, I'll get a room at the nearest five-star hotel with a huge bathtub and fluffy white robes to wear. Will that make up for skipping it today?"

Virgie got out of bed and stretched. "I'll hold you to that."

Phyl picked up the slacks and shirt she'd abandoned the night before and pulled them on, then headed toward the bathroom. She paused as she neared the dresser, the framed poem catching her attention. She cocked her head as she reread it. Then, the significance of the fourth line hit her.

"Oh, my God." She grabbed her shoes and forced her feet into them.

"What?" Virgie asked as she slipped her feet into a pair of sneakers.

"The next line in the poem. It's Theo. They were going to chop wood this morning." She was halfway out the door. "We have to hurry."

They raced down the hall. When they reached the stairs, they saw Emery walking in the front door.

"I didn't think anyone else was up," Emery said, pulling off her raincoat. "I went to the other side of the island to check my phone."

"Where's Theo?" Phyl demanded as they hurried down the stairs.

"I haven't seen them. The sofa's empty, and the blankets are folded. They must be around somewhere."

"Oh, my God, no!" Virgie screamed as she pointed at the little figurines. There were only six.

At Virgie's scream, the sound of doors being flung open and feet scurrying above them could be heard.

Joan was the first down the stairs. "What in the name of God is going on?" she demanded.

Virgie pointed to the figurines.

"Oh, no." Joan lowered her head.

Willie and Catherine arrived at the same time.

"Oh no, what?" Willie asked, looking from Virgie to Phyl.

"Another figurine is missing," Phyl said. "It's Theo."

"They're not on the sofa?" Willie glanced to the front room.

Emery shook her head.

Virgie turned on Emery in barely controlled rage. "It's you. You did this. You were outside," she yelled. "Where's Theo? What did you do?"

Emery stood frozen like a deer in the headlights. Five sets of angry eyes stared at her, waiting for an answer.

"I didn't do anything. I haven't seen Theo. They weren't here when I came downstairs. I went out the front door and didn't see them anywhere."

Phyl took charge. "All right, Virgie and I will go out the back and look. Joan and Catherine, you go out front. Willie, will you stay here with the doctor?"

"Seriously? You're not going to let me help?" Emery crossed her arms.

"Right now, you're the prime suspect. You're staying here where Willie can keep an eye on you."

"Fine, can I at least make coffee?"

"Knock yourself out," Phyl said, pulling on a coat.

Virgie and Phyl found Theo's body as soon as they rounded the back of the house. They lay face down on the ground next to an ax and a pile of chopped wood, their head covered in blood and their left arm nearly severed. Blood was everywhere.

Virgie's stomach revolted, and she fought the urge to throw up.

"Someone snuck up and attacked them. Just like Darcy," Phyl said. "Well, now I know for sure you're not the killer." She gave Virgie a half-smile.

Tears streamed down Virgie's face. "I could say the same about you."

"Were you worried it might be me?"

Virgie shook her head. "No. Not for a minute."

Phyl put her arms around the younger woman and pulled her close.

"Theo didn't deserve to die," Virgie cried into Phyl's shoulder.

"None of them deserved to die," Phyl said as she rubbed Virgie's back.

Virgie looked up. "We'll make it off the island alive, won't we?"

Phyl let out a long breath. "We're going to do everything we can to protect ourselves, even if it means locking ourselves in a room until somebody comes to get us."

Virgie let go and walked around the body and the blood. "Phyl, look." She pointed at the ground; a few feet from the woodpile lay a small ax, the head and handle covered in dark red blood.

"Any of the others could have swung that. It couldn't weigh too much."

Phyl nodded. "Even Catherine would have enough strength."

"But Emery is the most likely, don't you think? I mean, we saw her coming in the front door. It's almost like she was caught in the act."

"She's the most obvious, but I guess it's possible that one of the others snuck out before we came down, did this, and snuck back in. If Emery was on the other side of the island checking her phone, as she claims, she wouldn't have seen them."

"Whoever it was would have blood all over them. They'd have had to change clothes and shower."

"And get rid of the bloody clothes," Phyl said. "They wouldn't have had much time."

As she said that, Joan and Catherine came around the corner of the house and stopped abruptly. Catherine gasped. Joan bent over and vomited.

"Oh, no. The poor soul," Catherine said as she made the sign of the cross over her head and chest.

"I thought it was all God's plan," Virgie goaded her.

Catherine glared at her. "It is. But that doesn't mean I have to like it. Theo was a kind soul."

Joan wiped her mouth with the sleeve of her coat. "Yes, they were." She looked from Phyl to Virgie. "Any idea what happened? I doubt Theo accidentally hit themself on the head with the ax."

Phyl pointed to the small ax a short distance away. "Someone came up behind them and hit them with that." She looked at Catherine for a reaction, but the woman's demeanor and expression remained neutral.

A guilty person might feign anger or outrage. But she's not any of those things. She's unfazed, calm even. Virgie narrowed her eyes and stared at the woman, unable to decide what Catherine's true feelings were. She just stood there, emotionless.

"It doesn't look very heavy. I think it would be easy for anyone to swing it hard enough to do this," Joan said.

Virgie stared at Catherine. "We thought the same thing."

"Stop looking at me!" Catherine shouted, clenching her hands into fists.

Virgie's eyebrows raised. *Finally, some emotion.*

"I was sound asleep until someone screamed."

"So you say," Virgie sneered. "Maybe you snuck out earlier, did this, and snuck back upstairs."

Catherine glared at Virgie, her face growing red. "That's ridiculous. And it's just as likely you did this. Do you have an alibi?"

Virgie looked at Phyl, gave her a small smile, then looked back at Catherine. "Actually, I do. It's none of your business, but Phyl spent the night in my room. I was never alone."

Both Catherine and Joan looked at Phyl. "Is that right, Phyl?" Joan asked.

Phyl nodded. "Yes. Virgie hasn't been out of my sight since we left the front room last night. This morning we came downstairs together."

Virgie crossed her arms. "Emery saw us when she came in the front door."

"Emery was already up and outside?" Joan asked.

"Yes. She said she'd gone to the other side of the island to see if her cell phone had reception," Phyl said. "According to her, it didn't. We were on our way to look for Theo when Virgie saw a figurine was missing and screamed. You know the rest."

Catherine narrowed her eyes and glared at Virgie. "You could have snuck out while Phyl was asleep."

Phyl shook her head. "I'm a very light sleeper. I would have woken up."

Joan's forehead wrinkled. "Why were you looking for Theo?"

"The next line of the poem," Phyl said. "'Seven little castaways chopping up sticks; one chopped themselves in half, and then there were Six.'"

"I don't understand," Joan said.

"Last night, Theo said they were going to chop wood this morning. When I realized what would happen, we ran downstairs to find them."

"Oh my God." Joan ran a hand through her disheveled hair. "Tamara died just like the first line. Rosie, like the second line. Then Darcy, the same as the third line. Now Theo."

"I think we can say for sure that none of them were accidents or self-inflicted," Phyl said.

"Agreed." Joan nodded. "I suppose we should cover the body and move it somewhere before it starts raining again. Maybe the shed? It's close."

"Maybe there's a tarp we can use in the garage or the shed. I'll look," Virgie offered.

"Phyl, I'll go ask Willie to help you," Catherine said.

As Joan and Catherine started to walk away, Virgie called out, "We have to get rid of all the knives."

Joan turned to look at her; her eyebrows pushed together in a question. "What? Why?"

"The poem. Don't you remember? The next line…" She looked at each of them like they were idiots. "The next line of the poem!"

The three of them shook their heads.

"Oh, my God, how could you not remember it? 'Six little castaways playing with knives; one got careless, then there were Five.' That's how the next one will be killed."

After Phyl and Willie carried Theo's body to the shed, they returned to the pile of chopped wood. Each picked up as much as they could, took it into the front room, and dropped it in the box next to the fireplace.

"I'd like to think we're getting off this island today and won't need to use it," Phyl said.

"I hope so too. All of this is too much for my nerves," Willie said, brushing small pieces of bark from her sweater.

A small laugh escaped Phyl. "Sorry. You give off a tough-as-nails cop vibe."

Willie shook her head. "No, not anymore. I'm retired and not as young as I used to be." She sat on a stool at the bar. "I don't miss being a cop."

"Really?" Phyl asked.

"Yeah. It's gotten out of hand. Thugs outnumber the cops a thousand to one. And our hands are tied. Nowadays, criminals have more rights than the cops. If a cop makes even the smallest mistake, the press is all over it. Criminals are glorified, and cops get treated like scum." She crossed one leg over the other. "I'd much rather mind my own business and spend time with my grandkids."

Phyl looked at her in surprise. "You have grandkids?"

"Don't look so shocked. I was young once. I married a guy I met in college. It was a mistake, and we divorced two years later. I'd gotten pregnant right away, though. My daughter's name is Alice. She has twin boys, Danny and Peter."

"How did you attend the police academy with a kid?" Phyl asked.

Willie took a seat by the window. "My ex was a good father and helped out. After the divorce, Alice and I moved in with my mother. Once I was hired full time, I could afford preschool and daycare."

"I have to give you a lot of credit. It couldn't have been easy."

"No, it wasn't." Willie paused. "That's why it's so crazy that anyone could think I could kill someone."

Phyl looked at her questioningly.

"I'm a mother and a grandmother. It's just unimaginable that I would hurt someone, let alone kill someone."

"But you do have a gun," Phyl pointed out.

"Yes, but it's for self-defense. That's different," Willie said, patting her side where she carried the concealed weapon.

"Who do you think it is? Emery or Catherine?" Phyl asked.

Willie leaned forward and rested her elbows on her knees. "I don't think we should so fast to rule out Joan. She's one cold bitch."

"But she does have an alibi," Phyl reminded her.

Willie shrugged. "It could be either one. The doctor had the means and the opportunity. Who knows what she's got in that medical bag. But Catherine is a freaking nut case."

"I have to agree. She's wound so tight you could spin her like a top."

"Exactly. She's a religious zealot. She's so far gone I don't think she knows what religion she is. One minute she preaches like a Southern Baptist, the next, she's crossing herself like a Catholic. She's looney."

"That doesn't necessarily make her a killer," Phyl said.

"No, but she's definitely unbalanced, and in my professional opinion, that makes her dangerous."

"Not all mentally ill people are dangerous," Phyl pointed out.

"You're right. Most aren't. But four people are dead, and she's out of her gourd." Willie cocked her head to the side. "There's an old saying among cops: 'if it walks like a duck and talks like a duck—it's a duck.'" Willie chuckled. "I'm tellin' ya, Phyl, she's a duck."

CHAPTER ELEVEN

In the kitchen, Joan tended to the scrambled eggs on the stove. Catherine sliced a grapefruit in half with a sharp, serrated knife. Virgie placed two slices of bread in the toaster, never taking her eyes off Catherine and the knife. *Six little castaways playing with a knife.* Why hadn't anyone agreed with her to round up all the knives and toss them off the cliff into the ocean? The weapon used in the next murder was going to be a knife. *Why aren't we getting rid of them?*

"Virgie!" Joan said, getting her attention. "The toast, it's burning."

Virgie popped the toast up. "Sorry. My mind wandered for a minute." She put two more slices in the toaster and tossed the burnt ones in the trash. "I'm really uncomfortable with Catherine holding a knife."

Catherine turned to face her, holding the knife up in front of her. "Don't be ridiculous. I would never kill someone with a knife."

Joan and Virgie looked at each other and then at Catherine, unsure they understood what she meant. "But you'd kill using some other method? A knitting needle, maybe?" Virgie finally asked.

Catherine set the knife down on the counter. "Don't be ridiculous. The Bible clearly says, 'Thou shalt not kill.' It's a mortal sin."

"But your mother!"

Catherine stared at Virgie, her expression neutral. "That's different. She sinned against God."

Virgie's mouth hung open. She looked at Joan, whose eyebrows were knitted together in confusion, then turned back at Catherine. "Regardless of how you justify your mother's death, I'd feel a lot safer if we got rid of the knives."

"You're right," Joan said. "After breakfast, we can round up all the knives and throw them into the ocean."

Without turning around, Catherine asked, "How will we prepare meals? Have you thought of that?"

"Good point," Virgie said. "We could keep a small one and get rid of the others."

"There's a lock on that drawer." Joan pointed to the drawer closest to the sink. "The key is probably on Theo's key ring. We could keep the knife locked up."

"Who do we trust with the key?" Virgie asked.

"I'd say you or Phyl. It seems the two of you have a solid alibi for Theo's murder," Joan said. "I'd be willing to trust you."

"All right. Let's talk it over with everyone at breakfast," Virgie said.

Minimal conversation took place at the breakfast table, each lost in thought. Five of the six sat quietly, trying to decide who could be trusted and who was a killer. The sixth ate without fear or regret, sure that her actions were justified.

Finally, Joan spoke up. "I'm in agreement with Virgie. We should gather up all the knives but one and throw the rest off the cliff. We can keep a small one for preparing meals. One of the drawers in the kitchen has a lock on it. We can keep it there."

Emery wiped her mouth and placed her napkin on the table. "And who do we trust with the key?"

"I suggest Virgie or Phyl. They have a solid alibi for Theo's murder. Unlike the rest of us," Joan said.

"I'm fine with the plan. No sense leaving them around for the murderer," Willie said, then took a bite of her toast.

"I left Theo's key ring on the dresser in their room. I'll go get it," Phyl volunteered.

Virgie stood up. "All right, let's clear the table and collect the knives."

No one saw the killer slide a knife off the table and into her pocket.

After the knives were collected, the six assembled at the front door to walk to the cliff. The rain had subsided, but the temperature had dropped, and a thick fog had rolled in off the ocean.

As they headed out the front door, Joan announced she was staying behind to have a smoke. "I'll be the only one here. I'll be fine." She took out a pack of cigarettes from her coat pocket. "I'll wait here on the terrace." No one objected since the rest would be together on their walk to the cliff.

As they headed off into the fog, Phyl pulled the hood of her coat down over her ears and shoved her hands deeper into her pockets.

"I can't see three feet in front of my face." She took her cell phone out of her pocket, tapped the flashlight app, and pointed the light in front of her. "It doesn't help much, but it's better than nothing."

"Shit, why didn't I think to bring my phone?" Virgie grumbled.

Phyl grabbed her hand. "Stay close."

A few feet behind them, someone stumbled. "Shit," someone cursed.

Phyl looked back over her shoulder, but the fog was too thick to make out who it was.

"You okay back there?"

There was a pause, and then Willie answered, breathing heavily, "Yeah. I'm okay. I tripped over something and went down."

"Are you hurt?"

"No, just scraped my hands."

Phyl frowned. "Do you need any help?"

"No. It's only bleeding a little bit. Let's get this over with. It's freezing out here."

The three started walking again. The fog grew thicker, and the light from Phyl's phone only showed a few feet in front of them. Willie stumbled again. She grabbed onto Phyl's shoulder to keep from going down.

"Damn it!" Willie cursed. "Sorry, Phyl, I tripped over a branch or something. It's a minefield out here."

"Yeah, and this fog doesn't help."

The three soon caught up with Catherine and Emery, who hadn't noticed they'd fallen behind. As they neared the edge of the cliff, the fog began to lift, and they could see the ocean in the distance. They assembled near where Darcy had been standing only yesterday.

Phyl looked at Virgie. "Go ahead. Throw it out there."

Virgie pulled her arm back and, like pitching a softball, heaved the pillowcase full of knives as far out into the ocean as she could. The white pillowcase sailed eerily for a few brief seconds, like a ghost in the fog, then gravity took over, and the sack, like deadweight, plunged into the sea below.

Virgie turned to Phyl. "I feel a little better now."

"Good, me too." She looked at Willie. "How's your hands?"

Willie held up her right hand; there was a gash in the palm, and blood ran down her wrist. "I must have landed on a stick or something."

"Let me have a look," Emery said, taking Willie's hand and examining the cut. "It definitely needs to be cleaned out and maybe a stitch or two. I'll take care of it as soon as we get back."

Willie squinted at the doctor. "Okay, but in front of the others. I don't want to be alone with you." She looked around the small group. "Or any of you, for that matter."

Phyl nodded. "I think we all feel that way. There's safety in numbers." She took Virgie's hand. "Let's head back."

The fog had lifted somewhat, but the walk back was slow going. No one wanted to risk falling as Willie had.

By the time they were in sight of the house, the fog had thinned enough to see the portico that covered the front terrace. It was eerily quiet except for a gull screaming in the distance. Joan was nowhere in sight.

As they approached the terrace, Phyl saw the overturned lounge chair and walked toward it. Blood was everywhere. Joan lay face down behind it, her profile to the side, a deep gash in the side of her neck. Both of her hands were coated in it. She must have tried to stop the flow of blood as it drained from her body.

Virgie's delayed scream pierced the air and sent a chill down all but the killer's spine. "No!"

Emery and Willie rushed over, both slipping in the blood. Willie put her hands out, stopping herself from completely falling to the ground but covering both her hands in Joan's blood. Emery knelt by the body. There was nothing she could do. The killer had stabbed Joan in the throat, severing an artery. A serrated knife covered in blood lay nearby.

"Oh, my God!" Virgie's knees buckled, and she dropped to the ground. "Just like the poem."

"You had the key," Willie screamed at Phyl as she wiped her bloody hands on her coat. "It's been you all along."

"No." Virgie shook her head. "That's not possible. She was next to me the whole walk to the cliff. And she was with me when Theo was killed, remember?"

"She could have snuck out and killed Theo while you were still asleep," Willie pressed.

Virgie turned to Emery. "How long do you think Theo was dead before we found them?"

"Hard to say. But based on the color of the blood, I'd say less than an hour."

Virgie turned back to Willie. "We were awake for at least forty-five minutes before we came downstairs. Phyl couldn't have done it."

"Then who did?" Catherine looked from person to person.

Phyl reached into her pocket and pulled the key out. "The knife we saved is in the drawer." She held the key out to Emery. "Go check for yourself."

Emery nodded. "I'll be right back." The remaining women stood frozen in place, staring at Joan's lifeless body.

Two minutes later, Emery returned. "She's right. The knife is still in the drawer." The five stared at each other, knowing that one of them was a murderer and one of them her next victim.

Virgie choked back a sob. "I can't believe this happened."

"I'll see if I can find a tarp in the garage," Emery volunteered. Phyl and Willie nodded.

"There's so much blood." Virgie squeezed her eyes shut. "I'll never be able to forget the smell."

"Why don't you and Catherine go inside? Willie and I can take care of Joan's body," Phyl said.

Virgie shook her head vigorously. "No way I'm going to be alone with her." She stared at the older woman.

Catherine stood ramrod straight, her chin raised. "You can't possibly think I did this to her. I was with all of you the whole time."

Virgie glared at her. "The fog was so thick you could have turned back, done this, and rejoined us before anyone noticed."

Emery returned from the garage with a blue tarp and handed it to Phyl, who unfolded it and placed it on the ground next to Joan's body. "Doc, why don't you, Catherine, and Virgie go inside? There's no need for all of us to be out here in the cold."

Emery nodded. "How about I make some tea?"

Catherine smiled. "Yes, I could use some."

"A large glass of scotch sounds better," Virgie said. As she turned to go inside, she paused next to Phyl. "Watch your back," she whispered.

Phyl nodded. "I will."

Willie and Phyl carried Joan's body to the shed rather than bringing it into the house. When they were done, they changed out of their bloody clothes and joined the others in the front room. The fog had cleared, but the sky had darkened. It had begun to rain again, and the wind howled eerily through the trees.

Phyl collapsed on the sofa. "I wish we'd gone to the other side of the island and checked our phones before coming in. We won't get another chance tonight."

"Joan's murder shifted our attention to other things," Emery said.

Willie opened a new bottle of scotch, poured the liquor into three glasses, and handed one to each woman except Emery and Catherine, keeping one for herself. "This is a fucking nightmare." Willie pounded her fist on the bar and then took a large swallow of the amber liquid.

No one argued.

"Another figurine is missing. There's only five now," Virgie reported, her eyes narrowed as she focused on each of them in turn.

No one said a word as the four of them waged an internal battle with the panic that grew inside. The fifth smiled to herself. Things were going just the way she'd planned.

Outside the house, the storm intensified, and the rain pelted the windows harder.

"What was the next line of the poem?" Emery asked no one in particular.

Virgie raised her head to look at her. "'Five little castaways headed out the door; one stayed behind, and then there were Four.'"

There was silence again, everyone lost in their own thoughts.

"We need to get rid of that knife," Virgie said. Heads nodded.

"And while we're at it...Willie, the gun needs to go, too," Phyl said.

Willie's eyes narrowed into slits. "No fucking way are you taking my gun. I have the right to protect myself."

"All right, how about you keep the gun, and I keep the bullets?" Emery suggested.

"That's ridiculous. What am I supposed to do—throw the gun at the killer?"

"Where's the gun now?" asked Phyl.

"In the desk in my room," Willie said. "What about the doctor? She probably brought all kinds of drugs with her. If you want to take up my gun, I say the drugs go too."

Emery slowly nodded. "I'm okay with that as long as we can get to them if there's a medical emergency."

Willie stood. "I'll go get the gun."

Virgie stood also. "Considering the next line of the poem, I think we should all go with you."

"You're right. We'll all go," Phyl said.

The five mounted the stairs in a single file, except for Phyl and Virgie, who brought up the rear, shoulder to shoulder. At the top, they turned right and walked down the hallway. Willie stopped in front of the second door and unlocked it. She entered the room, went to the desk, and opened the drawer. She looked up at the others, her eyes wide. "It's gone."

Emery pushed Phyl and Virgie aside and closed in on Willie, her face twisted in rage. "What did you do with it?"

Willie's mouth opened and closed several times before answering, "I left it here. I swear I did."

Emery rushed at Willie, but Phyl grabbed her by the arm before she could hit the other woman. Emery struggled to pull her arm away, and Phyl had to wrap both arms around her waist to hold her back.

"Emery, stop. Stop it!" Phyl yelled.

Emery continued to wrestle against Phyl's restraint. Her face glowed bright red, and her eyes bulged. "Let me go! Let me go! She's the killer! We have to stop her!"

Catherine stood in the doorway, as still as a statue, eyes unblinking, staring at the chaotic scene in front of her. Her hand went to her throat, and she gasped for air before she sank to the floor.

"Phyl! It's Catherine. She needs help."

Phyl let go of Emery, who rushed to Catherine, crumpled on the floor. She knelt next to her and placed her face next to Catherine's. "She's breathing. Help me get her to the bed." Phyl helped Emery lift the older woman and carry her to the bed.

Emery sat on the edge beside Catherine and placed two fingers on Catherine's wrist, feeling for a pulse. "Her pulse is steady and strong. I think she just fainted." She looked up at Virgie. "Can you go to my room and get my medical bag? Here's the key. It's in the closet." She reached into her pocket and pulled out the brass key.

"You're not going alone," Phyl said. "Can you two refrain from killing each other until we get back?" She looked from Emery to Willie.

"I didn't attack anyone," Willie huffed. "But if you're that worried, I can go with Virgie, and you can stay here."

"No!" Phyl said a little louder than she intended. "No. One of you three is a killer. I'm not leaving Virgie alone with any of you."

Willie plopped onto the chair near the desk. "Have it your way."

Phyl looked at Emery. "You'll behave?"

"Yes, of course. Just go," she said as she raised one of Catherine's eyelids to check her pupils.

Phyl turned to Virgie. "Let's go."

They exited the room, leaving Emery and Willie to stare at each other.

Once in Emery's room, Virgie retrieved Emery's medical bag from the closet while Phyl opened each desk drawer. They were all empty.

"What are you doing?" Virgie asked.

"Might as well look around while we're here." Phyl smiled as she went to the nightstand and opened the drawer. "Who knows, maybe we'll find the missing gun." The drawer was empty.

Virgie went to the dresser, pulled out the top drawer, rifled through Emery's socks and underwear, and moved on to the other two drawers. "Nothing out of the ordinary here."

"Nothing here either," Phyl said from the bathroom. "Let's get back."

Virgie walked over to her and placed her palm on Phyl's cheek. "Thanks for looking out for me."

She covered the hand on her cheek. "I thought we were looking out for each other." She paused briefly. "Come on, let's get back."

Catherine was disoriented when she regained consciousness. She opened her eyes and saw the doctor hovering over her. Her first thought was that Emery was going to kill her. She screamed and pushed the doctor away. "What are you doing?" she demanded as she tried to sit up. "Get away from me!"

Emery placed a hand on her shoulder and pushed her back down. "You fainted. Lie back down. Virgie went to get my bag so I can listen to your heart."

Catherine pushed Emery's hand away and insisted on sitting up. "Get your hands off me. My heart is fine."

Emery stood. "I understand you're hesitant to let me examine you, but you fainted. You really should at least let me take your vital signs."

Phyl and Virgie appeared at the door, the doctor's bag in hand.

"Here you go, Doc." Phyl handed the black bag to Emery.

Catherine stood unsteadily. "I said you're not touching me."

"What's going on?" Virgie asked.

Emery frowned. "Catherine's worried I might kill her."

"Catherine, we're all here. No one is going to kill anyone. At least not right this minute. Let the doc take a look at you." Phyl's voice was soft and reassuring. "Please, sit back down."

Catherine's eyes narrowed as she looked at each person suspiciously. "I suppose it's safe with everyone here." She sat back down on the bed.

Emery proceeded to take Catherine's vital signs as the others watched.

"Your heart sounds good," she said as she looked at the gauge attached to the blood pressure cuff. "But your blood pressure is slightly elevated. I guess that's to be expected, considering the circumstances."

"I'd bet all our blood pressures are elevated," Willie said.

"I'd like to retake it in a couple of hours," Emery said, removing the stethoscope from her neck.

Catherine huffed. "If we're both still alive, of course."

No one said a word, each knowing that she wasn't making a joke.

Phyl cleared her throat. "I suggest we search the entire house and outbuildings for the gun."

"I assume you took the liberty of searching my room while you were there?" Emery asked.

Phyl raised a shoulder. "It seemed like a good idea."

Emery crossed her arms defensively. "And you didn't find the gun, correct?"

"Correct." Phyl nodded.

Willie began, "You could have hidden it somewhere else—"

"And how did I get into your room? Tell me that. I'm a doctor, not a magician." Emery threw the stethoscope into her bag and glared at Willie.

"You could have lifted my key when I wasn't paying attention."

"I've had enough of this bullshit. I'm going downstairs." Emery slammed the bag shut.

"All right, let's all calm down," Virgie said. "I think the rain stopped. Maybe we should take a walk to the other side of the island and see if anyone can get a signal on their phone."

Phyl nodded. "I think that's a good idea. We can search when we get back."

Willie and Emery stared at each other. "I know it's you," Emery raged.

Catherine gave Emery a push toward the door. "Come on, let's take a walk. And on the way, we'll pray to God almighty that one of us can call for help."

Virgie looked at Phyl. "I hate that woman. But if praying gets us a signal, I'm all for it."

Phyl raised an eyebrow, then took her hand and turned to Willie. "Come on. No castaway stays behind."

The rain returned but was only a mild drizzle. The wind, however, roared across the island. Wrapped in hooded raincoats and rainboots, the five women walked into the wind, heads down, bent forward as they leaned into the constant gales. No one said a word, knowing it would be next to impossible to hear anything over the wind's banshee like cries.

They walked in a staggered line five or more feet apart. Willie, in the lead, carried an unopened umbrella and occasionally swung it about like a sword. Emery had found a sturdy stick and used it to help navigate the uneven path. Phyl had picked up a clublike branch and held it at the ready in her right hand. Sporadically, one of them would take out a phone and check to see if she had service. Each one, minus Catherine, would utter a curse as she shoved the useless cell back into her pocket.

After thirty minutes, they were almost halfway around the island, having decided to go further in search of a signal. However, even though the five of them had three different cell service providers, not one of them had service. An hour after leaving the house, they returned cold and exhausted.

"Before we go in, let's search the garage. We're cold and wet anyway," Phyl said.

Willie and Emery grumbled but followed. The garage was cold and the wind whistled through nooks and crannies everywhere. The small building was windowless, and the only light source came from the open door and a single overhead lightbulb with a pull cord.

"All right, let's get this over with and get back to the house where it's warm," Phyl said.

They made quick work of it. No gun was found and they returned to the house.

"I suggest we all get out of these wet clothes and make something to eat," Emery said.

"I'm going to my room and pray," Catherine said as she headed for the stairs.

"Knock yourself out," Virgie said over her shoulder as she took off her coat and hung it over the back of a chair. She turned to Phyl. "I'm gonna get a brandy and take it to my room, lock myself in, and take a hot bath."

Willie cleared her throat. "Why don't we all go to our rooms and meet in the kitchen in two hours. We should be able to come up with something for lunch that doesn't require a knife to make it," she said, pulling out an unopened bottle of brandy and holding it up for Virgie to see.

Virgie nodded. "Make it a double, please." Virgie watched her like a hawk as she opened the bottle and filled a glass half full. After pouring the drink, Willie pushed it across the bar.

"Anyone else?" Willie asked as she poured one for herself.

Phyl nodded and Emery shook her head.

Willie placed another glass on the bar and filled it halfway while Phyl watched her every move.

Catherine sat on her bed and leaned back against the headboard. Her Bible lay open on her lap, and she read out loud. "'…and I will visit, upon the inhabited Earth, calamity. And upon the lawless, their punishment, and will quiet the arrogance of the proud. And the loftiness of tyrants, will I lay low.'"

She closed the book, looked out the window, took a deep, calming breath, closed her eyes, and began praying, "The Lord is my shepherd…"

Down the hall, Emery opened her medical bag, took out several small plastic bottles, and looked at the labels. She chose the one labeled Valium and returned the others to the bag. She twisted the lid off the bottle and tipped it on its side until a small, yellow pill fell out.

The stress and anxiety of the murders was overwhelming. Her nerves were shot. She needed the relief she knew the little yellow pill would provide. If she was going to survive and make it off the island alive, she needed to focus. *Just one pill.*

At the other end of the hall, Virgie filled the tub with hot water and a lavender-scented bubble bath. Shedding her clothes, she climbed in and leaned her head back against the edge of the freestanding claw-footed tub. She closed her eyes and inhaled the lavender, letting her shoulders relax.

With the sound of clothes being dropped on the floor, Virgie opened her eyes. Phyl stood in the doorway, naked.

"Room enough for me?"

Virgie held out her hand. "Absolutely."

Willie paced back and forth from one end of her room to the other. She stopped occasionally to glance out the window at the growing storm and sip from the brandy snifter. *Where in the hell is the gun? Who the fuck has it?*

She picked up the half-empty bottle of brandy and refilled her glass, then resumed her pacing. Thunder boomed somewhere in the distance. The wind had increased over the past hour, causing the rain to thrash against the house. Lightening flashed across the black sky, catching her by surprise. For better or worse, no one was leaving the house or the island for the foreseeable future.

CHAPTER TWELVE

Sunday Afternoon

Having made grilled cheese sandwiches and tomato soup, no knives needed, the five women sat at the table to eat. Four feared they'd be the killer's next victim. The fifth put on a good act, pretending to be frightened. All five sets of eyes darted around the table, inspecting one another, looking for a clue. Who was the killer? Who would be the next victim?

No one talked as they ate. Besides the occasional sound of soup being slurped and the whipping of the wind against the house, the room was quiet. Nerves were frayed. Each one wondered if help would arrive before the killer struck again.

Catherine placed her spoon on the table beside her bowl and looked at the others. "I know it's rude to leave the table before everyone is done, but I have a headache. If you'll excuse me, I'm going to go sit by the fire."

"I can give you something if you like," Emery offered.

Everyone stared at her. Willie let out a laugh. Emery looked at her, hurt etched on her face. Her brow furrowed and her mouth trembled slightly.

Catherine wiped her mouth and stood. "No, thank you, Doctor. I have Tylenol in my bag. I'll take it now that I have some food in my stomach."

"I understand your reluctance to take anything from me, but I assure you, I take my oath to do no harm seriously."

Catherine smiled but it didn't reach her eyes. "I'm sure Dr. Jekyll said the same thing right before he turned into Mr. Hyde."

Emery looked down, shook her head, and looked back at Catherine. "Please let me know if you need anything."

Catherine gave Emery a curt nod and left the table. The other four watched her until she was out of sight.

Willie popped the last of her sandwich in her mouth and chewed before speaking. "If you ask me, she's the one we need to keep an eye on."

Virgie placed her napkin on the table and leaned back in her chair. "I agree."

"Why?" Phyl asked, stacking her empty bowl on top of her plate.

"Her twisted religious beliefs. We're all heathens and sinners, but she's a saint," Willie said.

"She has absolutely no remorse over her mother's death," Virgie said.

"That could be said for thousands of other people who ignore the plight of those around them," Phyl said. "That doesn't make them murderers."

"Then which of us do you think is the killer?" Willie asked.

Phyl looked from Willie to Emery. "It's either you or you." She pointed from one to the other.

Emery looked weary. "I'm sorry you think I could harm someone. I'm leaning toward Catherine myself. The woman's heartless. I suggest none of us turn our backs on her."

Virgie stood and started clearing the table. "We never did search the house for the gun."

"We should do it now," Phyl said.

"Do you really think the killer hasn't moved it?" Willie said with a frown. "Catherine's all alone. She could be hiding it as we speak," Willie said.

Phyl let out a sigh. "Maybe so but searching the house will give us something to do besides sitting around, staring at each other."

"I guess it's the next best thing since we don't have a television," Emery said.

"How should we do this?" Willie asked.

Phyl stood. "Someone needs to stay with Catherine while the other three go search," Phyl said.

"I say we throw the keys to those rooms where bodies are off the cliff when we're done," Virgie said. "So, no one can go back in them."

Everyone nodded.

"Who volunteers to stay with Catherine?" Phyl asked.

Virgie, Willie, and Emery looked at each other. "Can't be me," Emery said. "She thinks I'm the killer." Willie and Virgie looked at each other.

"Rock, paper, scissors?" Virgie suggested.

Willie let out a laugh and shook her head. "A child's game to decide who stays with the killer? Sure, why not."

"Best two out of three?" Virgie said, holding out her fist.

Willie shook her head. "One time for all the marbles." She held out her fist. "Ready?"

Virgie nodded. "One, two, three."

On "three," Willie displayed a flat hand, paper. Virgie kept her hand balled into a fist, rock. "Paper smothers rock." Willie smiled. "I win."

"You're not dead," Virgie said as she entered the front room and spotted Catherine sitting in front of the fire.

"Yet? That's what you meant, isn't it? I'm not dead yet?"

Virgie plopped down on a stool at the bar on the opposite side of the room. "I didn't think you would be."

Catherine turned to look at Virgie. "Why is that?"

"My money's on you."

Catherine's forehead wrinkled, drawing her eyebrows together. "I don't understand. Your money's on me for what?"

Virgie let out a laugh. "That you're the killer."

Catherine's eyes and mouth shot open. "You're taking bets on who the killer is?"

"No, of course not."

"But you think it's me?"

Virgie nodded.

"Then why are you here alone with me?"

Virgie crossed her arms. "I lost a bet."

Phyl, Willie, and Emery searched every inch of the kitchen, pantry, and dining room. They didn't find the gun, but the small knife was still locked in the kitchen drawer. After finishing the search downstairs, they headed to the second and third floors, leaving the front room for last.

When they reached the top of the stairs, Phyl stopped and faced Willie. "Show me your waist."

Willie's face screwed up in a question. "Why?"

"I want to make sure you don't have the gun on you. You could be wasting our time on a wild goose chase."

"Seriously?"

Phyl nodded. "Pull your shirt up and turn all the way around."

Willie did as she was told. "This is ridiculous," she said, holding up the bottom of her shirt and turning in a circle until she was facing Phyl again. "Satisfied?" she asked with a smug smile on her face.

"Pull up both your pants legs."

Willie put both her fists on her hips. "What?"

"You heard me. You could have an ankle holster."

"Jesus Christ," Willie huffed, then reached down and pulled up the bottom of each pant leg, revealing nothing but brown paisley socks. "There. No gun. Can we get back to actually searching now?" Her eyes narrowed, and her tone was mocking. "Or would you like to strip search me?"

"All right, let's check Rosie and Theo's room, then Tamara's, Darcy's, and Joan's," Phyl said as she headed for the stairs to the Roberts' room on the third floor.

As they approached the room, the pungent odor of death assaulted them.

"Wait, I'll be right back," Emery said without explanation as she ran back down the stairs. She returned shortly with an armload of towels. "The smell will be overpowering," she said, handing each of them a towel. "You'll need to cover your nose and mouth."

Phyl's eyes grew wide, and she fought down the bile that churned in her stomach. Turning to the door, she inserted the passkey in the lock and opened the door. Death filled the air. Breathing through the towel helped but couldn't totally filter out the smell of decomposition and made her eyes water. They quickly searched the room, avoiding the body on the bed. As they went to exit the room, Phyl mistakenly glanced at Rosie, now bloated and unrecognizable. The contents of her stomach threatened to erupt, and she hurried from the room and locked the door. Emery quickly rolled up a towel and shoved it against the bottom of the door.

They proceeded to Tamara's room, then Darcy's, then Joan's. They repeated the process but found nothing. Emery wedged towels under the doors as tight as she could get them.

They moved on to Virgie's room at the far end of the hall and let themselves in. Phyl blushed, remembering the bath she and Virgie had taken a few hours earlier.

Willie turned to face Phyl. "Considering your relationship with Virgie, I think you should wait outside and let us do this."

Phyl started to object but thought better of it. "All right, but keep the door open."

Willie nodded. "Emery, I'll take the bathroom. You take the closet. Then we'll check the nightstand and dresser."

Emery nodded.

Phyl observed from the doorway. She couldn't see Willie in the bathroom, but there was nothing she could do about it.

Five minutes later, Willie and Emery finished. "Nothing here," Willie said as she exited the room and Emery followed.

"You don't sound surprised," Phyl said as she closed the door and locked it.

"I'm not," Willie said. "We kind of already ruled her out, didn't we?"

Phyl nodded.

They crossed the hall, and Phyl unlocked the door to her room. "I'll wait out here," she said, crossing her arms and leaning against the wall.

Emery and Willie entered the room. Emery went to the bathroom and looked under the sink and behind the toilet. Willie looked under the bed and in between the mattresses. Emery exited the bathroom and went through the dresser drawers as Willie searched the nightstands and desk drawers.

"Nothing here," Emery said as she headed for the door. Willie followed, giving Phyl a forced smile.

Next, they entered Catherine's room. Inside, everything was as neat as a pin. Nothing was out of place. The bed was made, and the bathroom towels were folded as if they'd never been used.

Willie went into the bathroom and looked around. Emery headed for the closet. Phyl checked the nightstand, dresser, and desk. It was quick work.

"Nothing in the bathroom," Willie said.

"Closet's clean."

"Same with the nightstand, dresser, and desk," Phyl said.

They left the room and locked the door from the outside.

Next, they headed to Willie's room. Without a word, she unlocked the door and stepped to the side. "It's all yours," she said, motioning for them to enter.

Inside, it looked like a tornado had hit. Clothing and used towels lay everywhere. Several glasses from the bar sat empty on the nightstand and desk.

"Sorry about the mess. I wasn't expecting company."

Phyl and Emery didn't say a word. This time, Phyl searched under the bed, the nightstand, and the desk. Emery took the closet, bathroom, and dresser. They left the room, and Willie locked the door.

"You already searched my room, but I'm guessing you want to look around again?" Emery said.

Phyl smiled. "Better safe than sorry."

Emery walked two doors down the hall and unlocked her door. "Have at it. I'll wait out here."

Willie and Phyl entered the room. Willie headed to the bathroom, and Phyl to the closet.

When they were done, they searched the nightstand, dresser, and desk. After looking under the bed, Phyl motioned Willie over. "I don't see the medical bag anywhere, did you?"

"No."

"Emery, can you come here?" Phyl called out.

Emery stepped into the room. "Yes?"

"Where's your medical bag?" Phyl asked.

Emery pointed to the closet. "On the shelf. Why?"

"You're sure?" Willie asked.

"Yes, I put it there after I looked at Catherine." She walked to the closet and looked in.

"It's gone!"

CHAPTER THIRTEEN

The three women returned to the front room to find Catherine and Virgie staring into the fire, not talking.

Virgie was the first to look up. "Find anything?"

"No, but the doctor's medical bag is missing," Phyl said as she, Willie, and Emery headed for the mysterious room behind the bar.

Virgie stood and followed them. "Missing?"

Emery nodded. "I put it in the closet after I looked at Catherine earlier. It was there when I came down for lunch."

Phyl pushed open the hidden door behind the bar, and the four walked in. They each took one of the cabinets. Virgie's held only toilet paper. "Well, we won't run out," she said.

The cabinet Phyl opened held a case of cigarettes, the brand Joan smoked. "That's strange, don't you think?" Phyl asked.

"It's very strange," Emery agreed.

"If we'd seen that before Joan was killed, I would have thought she put them there. That she was the killer."

"I would have, too," Phyl said.

Willie's cabinet held bottles of alcohol, two flashlights and extra batteries, a case of matches, and a few blankets. "Nothing too unusual here," she said.

Everyone walked to the cabinet Emery was perusing. "It's just a bunch of odds and ends," Emery said. "Bars of soap, candles, a dozen towels, and washcloths."

Phyl rubbed the back of her neck as she walked from one side of the room to the other. "But no gun or medical bag."

Willie started to leave the room but stopped and turned to the others. "I doubt either will magically reappear."

"Why not? They magically disappeared," Virgie said as she walked over to Phyl and took her hand.

Emery joined Willie at the door. "I need a drink," she said.

Willie looked at her questioningly. "I thought you didn't drink."

"I can't think of a better time to start," she said as she stepped over the threshold. She stopped abruptly and placed a hand on the side of her neck. "Ouch, I think something bit me," she said just before her knees buckled, and she dropped to the floor.

Having heard the thump, Catherine hurried over. "What happened?" Seeing Emery on the floor, she clasped her hands together on her chest. "Oh, no."

Willie knelt, rolled Emery onto her back, and started to feel for a pulse but stopped and looked up at the three women. "There's a tiny dart in her neck."

"Like the kind you throw at a board?" Phyl asked.

"Sort of, but it's tiny. Like a blow dart." Willie pointed to the object sticking out of Emery's neck. It was red and less than an inch in length. The end was divided into four tiny yellow wings like a playing dart.

Virgie knelt on the opposite side and held Emery's wrist, searching for a pulse. When she couldn't find one, she raised one of Emery's eyelids. The eye was glazed over and vacant. She sat back on her haunches. "Oh my God, she's dead." Tears suddenly spilled down her cheeks.

Catherine lowered herself to the floor and began to pray.

"Where did the dart come from?" Phyl asked, glancing around the room and then inspecting the doorframe. Just inside the doorframe, about five and a half feet from the floor, someone had glued a thin, two-inch plastic tube. A short black wire stuck out the back end of it. The tube and wire were painted the same color as the wall to blend in.

"Somehow, she must have triggered it when she stepped over the threshold," Phyl said.

Virgie stood and looked at the device. "So, it could have been any one of us?"

"Why didn't it go off when I walked into the room?" Willie asked.

"I'm guessing it was activated when we walked in, and Emery stepped on something to set it off," Phyl said.

Willie's eyes grew wide. "It could've been me. I was going out the door but stopped to say something."

Phyl's face hardened and she narrowed her eyes. "Or you knew it was there, and you stopped to wait for one of us to exit first."

"Don't be ridiculous. I didn't kill her. I didn't kill anybody," Willie said as she stepped over the body and went to the bar. She grabbed a glass from under the counter and the half-empty bottle of scotch, pouring until the glass was half full. She picked up the glass and took several long swallows. "This is a nightmare," she said, setting the glass down.

"Come on, let's move her to her room," Phyl said. "Virgie, would you get one of those blankets from the cabinet to wrap her in?"

Virgie nodded. She retrieved a blanket and placed it on the floor next to Emery's lifeless body. She and Phyl rolled Emery onto the blanket, folded the top and bottom over her head and feet, and wrapped the sides around her. They left the dart in her neck. If the authorities ever showed up, they'd want it for evidence.

"Do you think the poison in the dart is the same as what the killer used on Tamara and Rosie?" Virgie asked no one in particular.

"Maybe. Probably. I don't know," Phyl said, shaking her head. "The only thing we do know for sure is that Emery isn't the killer. Which means one of them is." She looked from Catherine, still sitting on the floor behind the bar, her head bowed, rocking back and forth, and mumbling unintelligently, to Willie, who had drained her glass of scotch.

Willie slammed the glass down on the bar. "You know, I think the two of you are the killers. You're in it together." She pointed at Virgie and Phyl with one hand as she poured more scotch into the glass with the other. "I know I'm not the killer. And that poor woman…" She gestured to Catherine, still a mumbling heap on the floor. "Look at her. There's no way she's capable of planning this." She turned back to Phyl and Virgie. "So that leaves you two."

Phyl reached behind her back and pulled Willie's revolver from where she'd hidden it in her waistband under her sweatshirt. She pointed it at Willie. Her hand shook. She'd never held a gun before, let alone pointed one at somebody.

Willie's eyes grew wide with surprise. "You found it!" She flashed Phyl a smile that was just a little over the top. "Here, give it to me before you accidentally shoot someone." She held out her hand. "You look like you're going to pass out. You've never held a gun before, have you?"

Perspiration dotted Phyl's forehead, and she started to hyperventilate. Her heart pounded so loud she was sure Willie could hear it. Virgie put a hand on her shoulder. "You're okay. Take a deep breath."

Hearing Virgie's voice, knowing she was right beside her stopped the buzzing in her ears and her breathing slowed. She swallowed then nodded.

Willie dropped her hand and took a sip from the glass she held in her other hand. "Well, well, well. Aren't you the clever one," she sneered. "How did you find it?"

Phyl took a step closer and tightened her grip on the gun. "You moved the nightstand. I noticed the indentation in the carpet, so I stuck my hand under it and found it duct-taped to the bottom." One side of her mouth curled into a smile. "If you'd moved the nightstand back in place, I wouldn't have thought to look."

Willie's green eyes darkened. "My bad." She picked up the bottle of scotch and poured more liquid into the glass. "You're smarter than I thought you'd be. I thought Joan would be the last one standing." She stopped pouring and looked at Phyl. "I thought you'd be somewhere in the middle, around the fourth or fifth in line." She set the bottle down and picked up the glass."

A combination of anger and nerves caused Phyl's hand to tremble. "Why, Willie? Why did you want us dead? What did we do to you?" Her voice quivered despite her best efforts to stay calm.

Willie took another sip of scotch and glared at Phyl over the rim of the glass. "My grandson was on that school bus."

Behind Phyl, Virgie gasped.

Willie slammed the glass down on the bar. "He nearly died."

"It was an accident. Phyl didn't mean to hurt anyone," Virgie said over her tears.

Willie glared at her. "My grandson is paralyzed; he'll never walk again." Spittle flew from her mouth. Her head whipped from Virgie to Phyl, hate and anger rolling off her in waves. "A friend at the highway patrol let me read the investigation report. Your right front tire was bad and should've been replaced. He suspected that's why you lost control, but he couldn't prove it." Her face glowed red. "Your negligence almost cost my grandson his life."

The gun shook a little more in Phyl's hand. Bile rose in her throat, almost making her gag. "Willie, I'm so sorry." Tears fell down her cheeks. "It was a horrible accident."

Willie screamed as she grabbed the bottle of scotch and heaved it at Phyl, hitting her in the shoulder. The gun went off, the sound a deafening roar. Blood erupted from Willie's upper left arm. She grabbed the injured arm with her right hand and took off running.

Surprised by the blast, Phyl dropped the gun, and it went off again. The bullet shot across the room and hit the wall near the fireplace, leaving a small hole. Stunned, Phyl smashed her eyes closed and clamped her hands over her ears. She stood frozen, unable to comprehend what had happened.

Behind her, Catherine rocked back and forth, her mumbling turned to painful moans. She stared off into space, her eyes glazed over. Virgie stepped around her, retrieved the gun, and set it on the bar. Seeing Phyl's distress, she wrapped her arms around the woman's waist.

"Breathe," Virgie whispered. "You're okay."

After a few minutes, Phyl's breathing returned to normal, and her heart rate slowed. She dropped her hands to her sides, took a deep breath, and opened her eyes. Her mind reeled from the suddenness of what had happened. She pulled away from Virgie and looked at her. Virgie's mouth was moving, but the ringing in Phyl's ears made it almost impossible to hear anything. Phyl shook her head slightly, trying to clear it. Finally, the ringing subsided.

"Are you okay?" Virgie asked.

Phyl nodded, still trying to process what had happened. She rubbed her shoulder where the bottle had hit her. "I shot her, didn't I?"

"I don't think you meant to. She threw the bottle at you, and the gun went off." Virgie pointed to the path of blood that led to the front door. "She wasn't injured too badly. She managed to run off."

Catherine moaned behind them. "Can you help me up," she asked.

Virgie went over and took hold of the older woman's arm. Catherine leaned heavily on her as she tried to stand on shaky legs. "Thank you," she said, her voice barely above a whisper.

"What do we do now?" Virgie asked Phyl.

Phyl picked up the gun and stuck it in the back of her pants. "We should help Catherine to her room so she can lie down. Then we need to come up with a plan."

They helped Catherine to her room, poured her a glass of water, and waited outside her door until they heard the lock turn into place. When they returned to the first floor, Virgie checked the shelf where the little castaways rested. Only four remained.

"She couldn't have gone far. She came back and removed a figurine," Virgie said.

"How sick is that? She's shot but still sticking to her script."

"The next line in the poem is 'one bumped her head, and then there were Three.' Do you think she'll try to get close enough to hit one of us over the head?"

"There's no telling what she'll do. She's got a bullet in her arm. It must hurt like hell, but she still has use of the other one." Phyl knelt beside Emery's body. "I don't think we should risk carrying her upstairs. Let's move her in there." Phyl motioned to the small room behind the bar.

"Can we roll her onto a blanket and drag her in?"

"Good idea. I don't think I'm up to heavy lifting."

Virgie entered the small room and returned with a blue blanket. They unfolded it and laid it alongside the body, then gently rolled Emery onto it. They each took a corner near Emery's head and dragged her into the small room. On the way out, they shut the door behind them.

"I'm dead on my feet," Virgie said, then covered her mouth with her hand, her eyes wide. "I'm sorry, that came out all wrong."

Phyl ran a hand through her hair. "Don't worry about it. I'm exhausted too." She opened the small refrigerator under the bar and took out two bottles of water.

Virgie sat on a barstool and leaned her elbows on the bar, her head resting on her hands. "What's the plan?" she asked, taking the bottle of water from Phyl and unscrewing the top.

Phyl drank down half the bottle of water and then said, "We've got the gun, so we have the advantage. But there's only three bullets left."

"That's not very many."

"No, it isn't," Phyl agreed. "And who knows how long until help arrives. We need to be smart, not take any unnecessary risks." She rolled her neck from side to side. "We're both exhausted. I say we lock ourselves in a room, put a chair against the door, and take turns getting some sleep."

Phyl unlocked the door to her room, reached in, and flipped on the light. "After what happened with the dart, I think we should look for booby traps."

Virgie nodded. Before they entered, they inspected the doorframe. There was no sign of any darts.

Phyl closed the door and pulled the desk chair over to wedge under the doorknob.

Virgie knelt beside the bed and lifted the spread to look under it. "I have no idea what we should be looking for."

"I don't either. It's probably pointless, but let's at least look," Phyl called from the bathroom.

Virgie carefully opened the closet doors and looked inside. The only thing she found was Phyl's coat, a few clothes on hangers, and two pairs of shoes. On the shelf was an overnight case.

Phyl exited the bathroom and went to the windows, pulling open the drapes and looking behind them. She also made sure the windows were closed and locked.

"I don't see anything," Virgie said as she sat in one of the wingback chairs facing the window. The storm had run its course, and the sky was beginning to clear. The chirping of a bird could be heard in a nearby tree. To the west, the sun was low on the horizon; a palette of pinks, oranges, and purples filled the sky. "Under normal circumstances, I love watching the sunset."

Phyl walked up behind her. "Being stalked like prey changes things, doesn't it?"

Virgie turned her head to look at Phyl. "Thanks for that. Now I'll never get any sleep."

"I'll take the first watch. You get some sleep. I'll wake you in, say, four hours?"

Virgie got up and walked to the bed. "What will you do while I sleep?"

Phyl motioned to her laptop on the desk. "I think I'll try to write."

"Our situation would make a good murder mystery."

"But I'm no Agatha Christie."

"No, you're much better looking."

CHAPTER FOURTEEN

Monday Morning

When Phyl woke, the drapes were open, and dark clouds hovered in the distance. The door to the bathroom opened, and Virgie walked out, her hair wet.

"Good morning," she said. "I was just about to wake you."

Phyl swung her feet off the bed and stood. "Did you shower?"

Virgie shook her head. "No. I didn't want to leave you unprotected. I just got my hair wet and combed it out."

"Any sign of Willie?"

"Not a peep."

"I hate to even think what she's planning next," Phyl said as she walked into the bathroom and turned on the faucet.

"We should check on Catherine and make sure she's okay."

Phyl exited the bathroom and retrieved the gun from the nightstand. She shoved it in her waistband behind her back before pulling a sweatshirt over her head. The metal was cold against her skin, causing a chill to run up her spine.

Before leaving the room, Phyl looked down the hall. Willie was nowhere in sight. They walked down the hall to Catherine's door and knocked. She asked who it was before she opened the door. She looked like she hadn't gotten much sleep; her skin was pale, and her eyes were bloodshot.

"We're going to the kitchen. You should come with us and get something to eat."

Catherine nodded, picked her Bible up off the nightstand, and followed them down the hall.

In the kitchen, Phyl took charge of the coffeepot while Virgie scrambled eggs and made toast. They offered to share with Catherine, but she reminded them she drank tea, not coffee, and would prefer to make her own breakfast, untouched by anyone else.

"Of course, Catherine," Phyl said. "Given the circumstances, that's a perfectly reasonable thing to do."

Catherine returned from the kitchen with her tea and a plate of toast. She sat across the table from them.

"How did you sleep?" Virgie asked, not sure she cared, but being polite.

"Not well. Maybe I should have asked the doc—" She raised her head and looked at the couple across from her. Her eyes were as big as the plate that held her toast. Her mouth gaped, and her eyebrows merged. "It wasn't a nightmare, was it? The doctor's dead, isn't she?"

Her fork halfway to her mouth, Virgie stopped and set the bite of eggs back on the plate. "Yes, it really happened." Her voice cracked.

"I misjudged her," Catherine said. "I was sure she was the killer."

"Well, up until Emery was killed, I was sure you were."

Catherine's eyes grew dark. "I told you I could never kill someone. It's a sin."

Virgie leaned her head to the side and narrowed her eyes. "Except in cases of adultery?"

Catherine huffed and rolled her eyes but didn't argue.

Virgie picked her fork back up and took a bite of eggs. After she swallowed, she asked, "Where do you think Willie is?"

"There's two dead bodies in the shed, so she probably spent the night in the garage," Phyl said before taking a sip of coffee.

Catherine set her teacup down. "But where is she now?"

"Your guess is as good as mine."

"Was she badly injured?" Catherine asked.

Virgie shook her head. "The bullet grazed her bicep. There was a lot of blood, but she won't die from it."

"I think we should try our phones," Phyl broke in. "See if we can contact the authorities."

Virgie's eyebrows scrunched together. "What about Willie? She could booby-trap the whole place while we're gone."

Phyl paused to consider Virgie's concern. "I think we have to take the risk. We'll search the house when we get back."

Virgie didn't look convinced.

"We have the gun. We have the advantage," Phyl reminded her.

"Okay." Virgie nodded. "Catherine?"

"I suppose I could use some fresh air," she said. "Let me get my coat."

"I'll get ours," Virgie said.

"Thanks," Phyl said. "Let's hurry before it starts raining again."

By the time they set out, the sky had darkened considerably, and the clouds were menacing. The wind came in raging gusts on the verge of becoming a squall. They walked, bent forward against the wind, along the rain-soaked obstacle path. Puddles, some several inches deep, slowed them down. Virgie took out her phone and found no reception. After they trudged the length of a football field, Phyl tried her phone, but there was still nothing. They continued on, each repeating the process. Catherine and Virgie again had no luck. They were a third of the way around the island when Phyl saw her phone had one bar. "I've got it!" she yelled, dialing 911, but the call didn't go through. "Shit," she said, trying again. Again, it didn't go through.

"Here, try Frankie's number," Virgie said, handing Phyl a slip of paper. "I found it this morning in the drawer by the radio."

"Frankie?" Catherine said.

"The woman who brought us out here on the boat," Virgie said.

Phyl dialed the number and waited. It rang one time before the call dropped. "Damn it."

"Try again," Virgie and Catherine said in unison.

Phyl punched in the numbers again and waited. The phone rang one time and again dropped. "Shit," Phyl cursed, redialing the number.

Virgie held up her hand, fingers crossed. "Third time's a charm," she said.

"From your lips to God's ears," Catherine said.

The phone rang once, then dropped the call again.

Phyl looked at the two women, disappointment written on their faces. "It's not raining yet. Why don't we walk further and see if we can get a stronger signal?"

"God would want us to persevere," Catherine said.

Virgie let out a small laugh. "Well, let's not disappoint God."

They kept an eye on the service bars on their phones as they walked. Virgie and Catherine had Northeast Mobile service, and neither found a signal. Phyl, who subscribed to Go Talk-Now, continued to show one bar but couldn't get a call through. By the time they were three-quarters of the way around the island, that bar had disappeared, the sky had turned black, and it had begun to rain again.

"I give up," Phyl said. "Let's get back before the wind sweeps us off a cliff."

Catherine and Virgie nodded their agreement and hurried toward the house. Phyl brought up the rear.

Phyl entered the house first, the gun drawn. It was eerily quiet. She checked around the doorframe for another dart but didn't find anything. They made their way inside. The fire in the fireplace had gone out, and the room was cold.

"I'll get a fire started," Phyl said. "You two can go on up and get into some dry clothes."

"No way," Virgie said. "I'm not leaving you here alone. We have no idea where Willie is or what she's up to."

Having taken off her raincoat, Catherine eased onto the sofa, her Bible in hand. "I'll wait too."

"Is there enough wood?" Virgie asked as she knelt next to Phyl.

"I think so, but if we don't get off the island today, we'll have to chop more."

A few minutes later, the fire roared in the fireplace and the room began to warm. Phyl and Virgie stood with their backs to it, trying to warm up.

"Should we make some tea or go change first?" Virgie said.

Catherine stood. "As much as I'd like some hot tea, I think it best that we get out of these wet clothes."

"I agree," Phyl said, taking Virgie's hand, and the three trudged up the stairs.

When they got to the top, they turned left down the hall and stopped in front of Catherine's door. She unlocked it and pushed it open. Phyl checked around the doorframe, but it was clean.

"We'll knock on your door when we go back down. Don't leave your room until we come back," Phyl said.

Catherine nodded. "I'm going to take a bath to help me warm up."

"Okay, will forty-five minutes be enough time?" Virgie asked.

"Yes, that should be plenty," Catherine said, then stepped inside and closed the door.

They waited to hear the lock turn on the door before continuing down the hall. "I'll grab my clothes and change in your room if that's all right with you?" Phyl said.

Virgie nodded and waited while Phyl unlocked the door and checked around the frame before entering. The room looked like a tornado had hit it. Every drawer had been turned upside down and emptied, and the clothes in the closet lay in a heap on the floor.

"Well, it looks like Willie's been busy," Phyl said. "I don't see any blood anywhere. She must have found a way to bandage the wound on her own."

"What do you think she was looking for?"

"I don't have a clue." Phyl shook her head. "She has to be smart enough to know I wouldn't leave the gun behind." She shook her head. "Give me a minute to get some things together."

Virgie sat on the bed, and tears began to fall down her cheeks.

Phyl walked out of the bathroom and stopped. "Are you okay?"

Virgie looked up. "No. Not at all."

Phyl walked over and sat beside her, putting both arms around her. They sat huddled together without speaking for several seconds before Virgie said, "We've only been here for three days."

"It feels like forever, doesn't it?" She kissed the top of Virgie's head and rested her cheek there. "We'll make it off this island alive. Don't give up on us."

"I'm not," Virgie said, wiping tears from her face. "We need to get a move on. We told Catherine we'd be back in forty-five minutes, and I need a shower."

"You're right," Phyl said, giving Virgie one last squeeze.

Fifty minutes later, a knock sounded on Virgie's door. They were both dressed, but Virgie was still drying her hair.

"Catherine?" Phyl called out.

"Yes. It's me."

Phyl opened the door with a frown. "You shouldn't have left your room alone."

The older woman clutched her Bible to her chest. "God will protect me."

Phyl shook her head. "You haven't seen Willie, have you?"

"No."

"Okay, wait here, we'll only be a minute. Virgie's drying her hair."

Catherine let out a huff. "You said forty-five minutes. I'm going to make my tea." She turned abruptly and marched back down the hall.

"Catherine, you shouldn't go by yourself," Phyl shouted after her, to no avail.

Without turning around, Catherine said, "God is my shepherd. I shall not want. He…"

Phyl shook her head and closed the door.

Virgie walked out of the bathroom. "Was that Catherine?"

"Yes. I told her we'd only be a minute, but she marched off down the hall."

"Do you think—"

A scream cut her off. Then, several loud thuds echoed down the hallway.

"Oh no." Phyl ran to the door, Virgie right behind her. They sprinted down the hallway and stopped at the top of the stairs. A door slammed from somewhere in the back of the house.

Catherine's crumpled body lay at the bottom of the staircase, arms and legs splayed in unnatural angles, her Bible on the floor next to her. From the angle her head was positioned, it was clear her neck was broken.

"No, no, no!" Virgie screamed as she and Phyl rushed down the stairs.

Phyl reached the bottom first and knelt next to Catherine. As she pressed her finger against Catherine's neck to feel for a pulse, she noticed a small amount of blood had trickled out of her ear.

"There's no pulse," she said as she rolled Catherine onto her back and began CPR. Virgie put her hand on Phyl's shoulder.

"Her neck's broken, Phyl. She's dead. You can't save her."

Phyl sat back on her haunches and stared at Catherine's lifeless body. "Maybe it was an accident. Maybe she fell." She looked up at Virgie. Tears were welling in her eyes.

Virgie stood and walked to the dining room. On the shelf above the buffet, only three little figurines remained. She walked back to where Phyl sat on the floor.

"It wasn't an accident," she said. "Another castaway is gone. There's only three."

CHAPTER FIFTEEN

Monday Afternoon, Two O'clock

Virgie retrieved the blanket Theo had left on the couch, and they wrapped Catherine's body in it, placing her Bible on her chest.

"Let's move her next to Emery before Willie comes back from wherever she's hiding," Phyl said.

Phyl lifted the head and shoulders, and Virgie wrapped her arm around Catherine's feet.

"Do you think Willie will try to kill us at the same time or separately?" Virgie asked, breathing heavily from the exertion.

"Separately," Phyl said. "Except for Tamara, she waited until everyone was alone. And so far, she's followed the poem."

"I'm going to have nightmares for a long time."

They gently laid the body in the room behind the bar, next to Emery. "I don't think I'll ever sleep without a light on."

Virgie wiped perspiration from her forehead with the sleeve of her shirt. "I didn't like her. And for a while, I was sure she was the killer. She was a self-righteous, judgmental bitch. Why am I so angry that she's dead?"

Phyl had grabbed a towel from a cabinet and wet it in the sink behind the bar. "You're angry because you're a compassionate human being," she said as Virgie closed the door to the little room.

Virgie took the towel from Phyl and shoved it into the space between the floor and the bottom of the door to hold off the offending odor that would permeate the air if they were forced to stay on the island another day.

"I can't fucking believe this is happening," Virgie said as they walked to the kitchen. "What do you think Willie will do next?"

"I think she'll try to separate us," Phyl said, going to the sink and turning on the water.

"The next line of the poem is 'Three little castaways didn't know what to do; one got an idea, and then there were Two.'" She paused. "It's not very specific. She could try anything."

"We need to find her before she finds us," Phyl said, washing her hands. "No more cat and mouse."

"And what do we do when we find her? If we find her?"

"Shoot her if we have to," Phyl said as she dried her hands. "I'm not playing this game any longer."

Virgie's hand shook as she scooped coffee into the coffee maker and added water.

"Do you think she's watching us?"

"The thought of it gives me the creeps," Phyl said as she peeked into the dining room, then turned back to Virgie. "She might have installed cameras throughout the house."

Virgie dropped the mug she'd just picked up, and it shattered on the tile floor, sending shards everywhere. "Do you think she watched us…" Virgie looked at Phyl wide-eyed.

Phyl knelt, picking up the larger pieces of the cup. "I don't think we can rule anything out."

Virgie grabbed the broom from the corner near the back door and swept up the smaller pieces. "Phyl."

Phyl looked up. "Yes?"

Virgie stopped sweeping. "She has the doctor's medical bag. There could be hypodermic needles and drugs in it. And she might have the ax she killed Theo with."

Phyl stood and dropped the broken pieces of the mug into the garbage can. "There's not much we can do about the ax except not let her get close enough to use it. And with a bullet in her arm, she might not even be able to lift it." She walked over to the coffeepot and poured coffee into a mug. "As for the drugs and hypodermic needles"—she took a sip from the cup—"we don't eat or drink anything that's been opened. She could use a hypodermic needle to shoot poison into something, so we only eat canned foods."

"There's plenty of those in the pantry."

"No wine or liquor in a corked bottle. It'd be easy to stick a needle through one and poison it."

"We probably should avoid alcohol anyway. We need to keep our wits about us."

Phyl nodded. "If we have to stay another night, we take turns sleeping."

"Agreed. And we should try our phones again before it gets dark."

Phyl nodded.

Virgie scooped up the debris from the floor with a dustpan and emptied it under the sink. After returning the broom to the corner, she found two cans in the pantry. Holding them up, she asked, "How does tuna and peas sound?"

The rain was unrelenting, and coupled with gale-force winds, it wasn't safe to walk around the island to find cell service. They decided to hole up in Virgie's room because she had a better view of the front of the house. They carried a box of canned food, a can opener, water bottles, coffee, and the coffeepot upstairs. After they deposited the items in Virgie's room, they went across the hall to Phyl's room to gather her things, then returned to Virgie's room.

They sat quietly on the bed, each lost in their own thoughts. Phyl was the first to stir and walked to the window. "What do you suppose she's up to?"

"I don't know. Let's look out the backside of the house."

They walked across and opened the drapes in Phyl's room. They couldn't see anything or anyone.

"I wish we'd thought to grab the ax," Virgie said.

Phyl was silent for a minute, a pensive look on her face. She stood and went to the door. "I've got an idea." She removed the chair and unlocked the door. "Wait here. I'll be right back."

Virgie went to the door and watched Phyl jog down the hall to where a fire extinguisher hung. She pulled it loose and returned to the room.

"Good thinking."

"It's better than nothing." She placed it on the floor near the door. "I have another idea." She grabbed Virgie's hand and pulled her down the hallway. "Hurry."

Phyl led Virgie to the room behind the bar. They stepped over the bodies on the floor. "Grab the matches and washcloths," she said as she opened the cabinet that held the liquor bottles and grabbed several bottles of Irish whiskey.

"Molotov cocktails?" Virgie asked.

"Exactly." Phyl smiled.

They carried their supplies back to the room and began assembling a few "cocktails."

"I wish I'd talked to my grandmother more," Virgie said out of the blue.

Phyl looked up. "I thought they didn't approve of your lifestyle."

"My grandfather certainly didn't, but he's dead. My grandmother's still alive, but we're not close," Virgie said. "Maybe I should have tried to reconcile with her once he was gone."

"Virgie, you're talking like we aren't going to make it." She touched her cheek. "We're going to survive. As long as we stay vigilant, we'll be okay."

Tears escaped down Virgie's cheeks, and she wiped them away. "The rain's letting up," she said, turning to look out the window. "Should we walk to the other side of the island and try our phones again?"

"I don't think we should risk it."

"Okay." She turned back to Phyl. "I hope Frankie comes back soon."

"I hope Willie doesn't kill her if she does." Phyl raised her head. "Do you hear something?"

Virgie looked around the room. "No, but I smell something." She walked to the door and stopped. "I think it's smoke." She put her hand on the door, but it wasn't hot.

Phyl moved to the door and knelt, positioning her nose near the bottom of it. "It's definitely smoke."

"Is she crazy enough to burn down the house with us in it?"

"She's crazy enough to do anything."

"What do we do?"

"If we go out the door, she could be waiting for us."

"We'd probably be stopped by the fire, anyway."

"We could use the sheets to make a rope and go out the window."

"But she could be hiding out front. And I'm afraid of heights."

"She's probably expecting us to climb out this window. We could go out the window across the hall. We could climb down the big maple tree. It should give us some cover," Phyl said. She took both of Virgie's hands in hers. "I understand you're afraid, but I think it's the only way out."

"Shit, Shit, Shit!" Virgie chewed on her bottom lip. "Okay, let's do it."

Phyl released her hands and went to the door, slowly opening it and closing it when she saw the smoke-filled hallway. "I don't see any fire, just smoke. Can you grab two towels and get them wet?"

Virgie ran to the bathroom and returned with two wet pink hand towels. She handed one to Phyl and kept the other for herself.

Phyl quickly went to the desk, pulled the flash drive out of her laptop, and placed it in her pocket. "I don't want to lose all my work." She gave Virgie a half-smile before covering her nose and mouth with the towel and opened the door an inch, peeking out to look for Willie, who wasn't nearby. She took the gun from her waistband and held it at the ready. She crossed the hallway and unlocked the door to her room. As soon as it was open, Virgie hurried across the hall and closed and locked the door behind her. Virgie went to the window and looked through a tiny opening in the drapes. The rain had stopped.

"All right, I'll go first," Phyl said. "Once I'm clear, you climb out. But before you do, drop the fire extinguisher out the window. I'll get it when I get down."

Just as Virgie was about to close the drapes, Willie ran from the back of the house and into the shed.

"Shit, she just went into the shed," Virgie said.

"We need to get her back in the house. Out front would be even better."

"I could throw a bomb out of my window on the other side of the house. When she comes out to see what it is, I'll run back here and climb out."

Phyl thought about it. "All right, it might work. Just hurry once you throw it."

Virgie grabbed Phyl's arm. "Be careful."

Phyl nodded. "Take some deep breaths, and don't look down. You can do this," Phyl assured her before pulling away and going to the window.

Virgie hurried back across the hall.

"Okay, I'm ready," Phyl called out. "Throw the bomb as far as you can."

Virgie took a swallow from the bottle of whiskey, grimaced, then stuffed one end of a washcloth into it. She struck a match, lit the cloth on fire, wound up, and threw the bottle as far as she could. It landed on the terrace and burst into flames. The resulting boom was loud enough for Phyl to hear on the other side of the house. When she saw Willie run out of the shed, she quickly climbed out of the window and onto the nearest branch.

Virgie hid behind the drapes, waiting to see if Willie exited the house to investigate. She wasn't disappointed. When Willie appeared on the terrace, Virgie raced back across the hall, grabbed the fire extinguisher, and tossed it out the window. It landed with a thud and rolled close to the house. She slowly climbed out onto the ledge. Pausing to gather her courage, she closed her eyes and took several deep breaths. Once centered, she focused on the branch closest to the house. Phyl had already climbed a few feet down, and the limb was empty. Virgie plastered her back against the house. Her heart was racing; she moved her right foot over twelve inches and then her left. She wiped perspiration from her forehead, took another deep breath, and slid her foot another twelve inches, then the other. As she moved her foot one more step, she heard a low thumping sound off in the distance, like the thumping of a bass drum. *Oh, God, what now?* She quickly moved the rest of the way to the tree, climbed onto the vacated branch, and began her descent.

Phyl waited on the ground, the fire extinguisher in one hand and the gun in the other. When Virgie joined her, she handed her the fire extinguisher. In the distance, the thumping cut through the air like a sledgehammer, growing louder and more intense. "Do you hear that noise?" she whispered to Phyl.

Phyl nodded. "What is it?"

"I don't know, but I can feel it down to my toes."

They crept along the back side of the house, Phyl in front with the gun at the ready. Virgie followed close behind, the fire extinguisher in one hand and the nozzle in the other.

The unknown sound in the distance grew into a deafening roar, and a steel gray Coast Guard helicopter approached overhead.

As Phyl and Virgie crept to the corner of the house, Willie jumped out in front of them and flung the hatchet at Phyl with her good arm. It flew end over end. The wooden handle hit Phyl in the same shoulder as the bottle had, and the gun went off. The shot went wide, missing Willie, whose face contorted with rage. Phyl fired the gun again. Her hand shook so violently that the round missed its target. She barely had time to fire the last bullet before Willie, screaming like an injured hyena, tackled her to the ground. "Fuck," Willie yelled as she rolled off Phyl onto her back. Blood gushed from a hole in her thigh. She let loose a string of profanity as she tried to get up. Virgie pushed her back down and pointed the nozzle of the fire extinguisher at her.

"Stay down," Virgie screamed as the helicopter descended to the ground behind the house.

Willie fell back, clutching her thigh with both hands, trying to stanch the flow of blood. "Fuck you," she yelled. "Fuck you both."

Virgie looked at Phyl, who was slowly getting up. "Are you alright?"

Phyl rubbered her right shoulder. "I'll have a huge bruise."

"Better the handle hit you than the other end." Virgie tried to smile. "Help finally arrived." She nodded to the helicopter. "Better late than never, I guess."

As the rotor on the chopper slowed, two guardsmen jumped out, one of them armed with a handgun, and cautiously approached the women. Virgie set the fire extinguisher on the ground, and they both raised their hands.

"What's going on?" the guardsman with two thick stripes on his arm demanded.

"The bitch shot me," Willie screamed. "Twice!"

The two guardsmen looked at Phyl. "Where's the gun?"

Phyl pointed to the revolver on the ground a few feet away. "It was self-defense. The gun is hers. She's killed seven people. There's five bodies in the house and two in the shed."

The guardsman's eyebrows scrunched together. He turned to the man next to him. "Radio for another chopper and notify Captain Marshall of the situation."

"Yes, sir," the guardsman replied.

"And we need the medic."

"Yes, sir." The young man turned and hurried back to the helicopter.

"Is there anyone alive besides the three of you?"

Phyl and Virgie shook their heads. "They're all dead," Phyl said.

The guardsman blinked, then said something into his mouthpiece, then turned back to them. "As soon as the other units arrive, you'll all be taken to the base on Nantucket."

"Thank you," Virgie said, her voice choked with relief.

Phyl, her hands clenched into fists, looked down at Willie. "Did you really think you could kill all of us and get away with it?"

"I never intended to get away with it," Willie said through gritted teeth. "The last castaway dies too, remember?"

Phyl and Virgie stared at her. Phyl was the first to speak. "You were going to kill yourself?"

Willie nodded. "That's why I brought the gun."

"But what about your daughter and your grandkids?"

"My daughter hates me, and I haven't seen her kids in years."

"Not even the grandson who was injured?"

Willie shook her head. "She says I'm a bad influence."

Phyl dropped to the ground, exhausted. "I understand why you hate me, but why Virgie and the others?"

Before Willie had a chance to explain, the medic ran up, knelt, and quickly assessed the situation. "Two bullet wounds?"

Phyl and Willie both nodded.

"All I can do here is slow the bleeding. We need to get you to a hospital as soon as possible."

The medic cut away Willie's shirt sleeve and poured something on the wound. Willie screamed and fought to pull away. The medic took a hypodermic syringe and a small glass bottle from the backpack and filled the syringe with clear liquid from the bottle.

"What's that?" Willie demanded.

"Something for pain," the medic said as he pushed the needle into Willie's good thigh.

Willie hissed when the needle punctured her skin. Within a few minutes, she'd calmed down enough for the medic to continue.

Phyl stood. "Why, Willie? Why Virgie and the others?"

Willie glared at Virgie. "You let Kenny drown."

Virgie gasped; her knees buckled and she sank to the ground.

"Who was Kenny to you?" Phyl asked.

Willie let out a sigh. "His grandfather was my training officer when I joined the force. Joe had a massive heart attack a month after Kenny drowned. You killed him, too, as far as I'm concerned."

Virgie's chin dropped to her chest, and she began to cry.

"Willie, it was a horrible accident. Just like the school bus," Phyl pleaded. "Can't you see that?"

Willie pounded her fist on the ground. "No," she yelled at Virgie. "You weren't paying attention. You took your eyes off him."

Virgie looked at Phyl. "I only turned away for a second," Virgie said, barely above a whisper.

Phyl turned to Willie. "What about Catherine?"

Willie's attention was diverted by the medic, who poured the same substance on her thigh. "Fuck. You could have warned me," she yelled.

"Willie, what about Catherine?" Phyl persisted.

Willie lay back on the ground. "The man her mother had an affair with." She stared up at the sky. "He was my brother." She looked at Phyl. "They were in love. She was going to leave her husband and that crazy church. They were going to run away together."

"And Catherine found out and killed them?"

Willie nodded.

"So you killed her."

Willie smirked. "I think Catherine would call it an eye for an eye."

Phyl dropped to the ground next to Virgie. "And the others?"

"The judge humiliated me one too many times. She acted like she was God, like she had power over life and death."

"So you killed her?"

"It was the Sheldon case. She declared a mistrial and let him walk away. And he went out and killed those two little girls."

Phyl couldn't believe what she was hearing. "Do you not see the hypocrisy?"

"What are you talking about?"

"You're the one playing God. You appointed yourself judge, jury, and executioner."

Willie stared daggers at Phyl and Virgie while one corner of her mouth turned up in a sneer.

An hour later, Phyl and Virgie sat in the back of a Coast Guard helicopter, waiting to return to Nantucket. Willie had already been taken away on an earlier chopper. They watched the tendrils of smoke drift out from the upstairs windows. The guardsmen had put the fire out earlier and opened all the windows to let the smoke escape.

From her coat pocket, Phyl pulled a pint-size bottle of whiskey she had procured to make a bomb and handed it to Virgie.

"You think of everything," Virgie said, then took a swallow, wincing as it burned down her throat. She handed it back to Phyl, who took a pull. She wiped her mouth with the back of her hand and held it out to the guardsman seated across from her, who shook his head.

"Thanks, but I'm on duty."

CHAPTER SIXTEEN

Monday, Late Afternoon

Wrapped in gray wool blankets, Phyl and Virgie huddled together on a bench in the Coast Guard office on Nantucket Island. They sipped hot chocolate from black mugs adorned with the Coast Guard logo. The helicopter ride from the island to Nantucket had been surprisingly quick. Help had been so close, yet so incredibly far away.

A short woman in a blue camouflage uniform walked up and stood in front of them. "Excuse me," she said. "Would you please follow me?"

They were shown into a private office. Behind the desk sat a woman in a similar uniform, but several colorful medals adorned the left side of her chest. She stood when they entered and held out a hand.

"Ms. Long, Ms. Campbell. I'm Captain Marshall." She shook hands with both. "Please have a seat." She motioned to the two chairs in front of her desk. "The Nantucket police don't have jurisdiction of Castaway Island, so the State Police are on their way from the mainland. They'll be taking over the investigation. They'll want to interview you when they arrive," the captain said, taking a seat behind her desk.

"Captain, who sent the helicopter?" Phyl asked. "We hadn't been able to contact anyone. The radio was sabotaged, and we couldn't get cell service. We'd almost given up hope."

"You have Frankie Nugent to thank for that," she said.

"The woman who took us to the island?" Virgie asked.

"Yes. She's a reserve guardsman here. She joined right after she finished rehab on that leg. Tough as nails, that one. She was sure something was wrong. She pushed us to investigate when she didn't hear from anyone after seventy-two hours and got several dropped calls from an unknown number." The captain shook her head and smiled. "She wouldn't take no for an answer. She wanted to go, but the seas were too rough for her little pontoon boat, and considering the situation, it's a good thing she didn't."

"She probably saved our lives," Virgie said.

"While we wait for the state people, I can fill you in on what we know so far." The captain opened a file in front of her. "The suspect set a fire at the top of the staircase on the second floor."

"Her name's Willie. I mean Wilma Kerrel," Virgie offered.

The captain nodded. "It doesn't look like she intended to burn the house down. The wood was wet, so it caused a lot of smoke damage but didn't spread outside the initial area." She looked up at the two women. "I think she was trying to smoke you out."

"Well, it worked. She forced us out a window," Phyl said.

"We found five bodies in the house and two in a shed."

Both Phyl and Virgie nodded.

"Ms. Kerrel admitted to killing all of them. She didn't appear to feel guilty about any of it."

"She wanted to make us pay for past transgressions. I think she saw herself as some kind of avenging angel," Phyl said.

"She'd been a cop years ago and was dismissed for falsifying evidence," Virgie broke in. "I think that's when it started. She said bending the rules was justified to get the thugs off the street."

"Sometimes, no matter how hard we try, a few unbalanced people slip through the hiring process and end up in uniform. The damage they cause taints the whole system," Captain Marshall said.

"I'm sure there are more good cops than bad," Virgie said. "But we only hear about the bad ones."

"Sad but true." The captain paused briefly. "The seamen at the scene notified me that they found a journal in her coat pocket. She documented everything. It's as good as a confession. We'll turn it over to the state police when they arrive."

Phyl's shoulders slumped. The adrenaline that had coursed through her body earlier had worn off, and exhaustion took its place. She looked down at her hands clutched together in her lap and sighed. "I can't believe we all fell for the ruse." She looked at Virgie. "We were so naive."

The phone rang, and the captain picked up the receiver. "Yes, Ensign?" There was a pause. "Thank you. They'll be right out." She hung up the phone. "An officer from the State Police is here. They'll escort you back to the mainland." She reached out her hand. "I wish we could have met under better circumstances."

Virgie and Phyl shook the captain's hand. "So do we. Thank you, and please give Frankie our thanks. She saved our lives," Virgie said.

"You can thank her yourself. She's waiting outside."

When they exited the building, two women were waiting for them. Reserve Ensign Francine Nugent, now in a blue camouflage uniform, stepped forward and held out her hand. Virgie brushed it away and wrapped her arms around the taller woman, tears already falling down her face. "How can we ever thank you?"

Frankie returned the hug. "No need. I just wish we'd gotten out there sooner. I can't believe they're all dead." Her eyes welled with tears. "That sweet, young woman, Tamara?"

Phyl nodded.

"It's tragic. She was so full of life," Frankie said.

The other woman, in a blue business suit, cleared her throat. "Sorry to cut in, but we have a ship to catch." She held out her hand. "I'm Detective White with the Massachusetts State Police. I'll be escorting you to Boston. I'll also be overseeing the investigation. We already have a team on the way to the island." She opened the rear passenger door of a black GMC Yukon and motioned for them to get in.

Phyl and Virgie hugged Frankie one last time. Phyl handed her a business card.

"I'd like to stay in touch if that's all right with you."

"Absolutely," Frankie said, taking the card.

After they climbed into the back seat, the detective continued, "The Coast Guard has a ship going to the mainland, and they've offered us a ride, so we don't have to wait for the ferry."

The drive to the dock took less than ten minutes. As they walked to the gangplank of the USS Grand Isle, Phyl stopped. "Do I have time to make a phone call first?"

The detective nodded affirmatively. Virgie tilted her head in question.

Phyl smiled. "I need to make a reservation. I promised you a five-star hotel with an extra-large bathtub, remember?"

EPILOGUE

March, The Following Year

Virgie walked into the kitchen just as Phyl hung up the phone. "Who was that?" she asked.

"Detective White. They've completed the investigation. She's close by and wants to stop in to update us before they hold a press conference tomorrow."

Virgie put her arms around Phyl's neck. "Hard to believe it's been six months."

Phyl put her hands on Virgie's hips and pulled her close. "It is," Phyl said as she leaned down and kissed Virgie's neck.

"I'm not looking forward to the press hounding us again," Virgie said.

Phyl leaned her head back and looked down at Virgie. "Maybe we should go somewhere. Hide out until the media circus dies down."

"Like an island somewhere?"

"No. Definitely not an island." Phyl shook her head as she resumed brushing her lips down Virgie's neck. "You smell so good," she whispered.

A knock on the front door stopped things from progressing any further. "To be continued," Phyl said as she released Virgie and left to answer the door. "Detective White, come in."

"Hello, Ms. Long. Ms. Campbell. Thanks for letting me stop by."

"Have a seat." Phyl motioned to the sofa.

"We were just about to have a glass of wine. Will you join us?" Virgie asked.

"I'm off duty. I'd love a glass."

"Red or white?" Phyl asked.

"Red, please," Detective White said, taking off her coat. She turned toward Virgie as Phyl left the room. "How are you doing?"

Virgie let out a long, slow breath. "We both still have nightmares; they call it survivor's guilt. But the counseling helps. I think. And we have a wedding to plan. That gives us something to focus on."

"When's the big day?"

"September second," Virgie said.

"It'll be here before you know it."

Phyl walked back into the room with three glasses of wine and handed one to Virgie and the detective before settling next to her fiancée.

"Thank you," Detective White said, taking a sip. "I wanted to give you a heads-up. We're holding a press conference tomorrow. We'll be releasing our findings, and it'll stir things up with the press."

"We're thinking about leaving town for a while," Phyl said.

"Not a bad idea," Detective White said, then paused to take another sip of wine. "So, here's what we've uncovered. First, it turns out that the mysterious Mr. Moore was, in fact, Wilma Kerrel. She'd had several undercover assignments and was adept at disguises."

"I'll be damned," Phyl said. "She had me completely fooled."

"That wasn't the only thing she was good at. She had quite a bit of money stashed away in the Cayman Islands, at least half a million."

"I'm guessing it came from sources other than her work at the PD?" Virgie asked.

"Exactly. She'd been taking cuts of money she'd seized from drug dealers, gangs, and gambling rings. The Irish mob was also paying her to give them a heads-up on criminal investigations. She'd been doing it for at least a decade. Eventually, she was forced to resign for falsifying evidence on the Buttons case."

"Incredible," Phyl said.

"We also figured out that she didn't own Castaway Island. There's a group of Japanese investors who intend to open a resort on it someday. Posing as Mr. Moore, she rented it for three months. She'd been planning this for over a year."

"We know why she chose seven of us, but what about Theo and Rosie?" Phyl asked.

"The elderly woman who died in their care was her mother. She believed they either killed or let her die on purpose."

"Why would they do that?" Virgie asked.

"She claims her mother kept a lot of cash in the house. After she died, it came up missing. The authorities cleared them, but Willie couldn't let it go."

"It's all so bizarre. What do you think triggered her? I mean, you don't wake up one morning and decide to round up a group of people and execute them."

The detective took a sip of wine before she continued, "By all accounts, she was a good cop the first five years of her career. She was even awarded the Medal of Valor for saving an elderly woman from a burning building. Then, one night, she and another cop were eating dinner in a coffee shop. A guy wearing a ski mask ran in, shot the other cop in the head execution-style, and ran out. They figured it was a gang initiation, but they never caught the guy. Willie was covered in blood and gore. That's when she started going downhill. She started taking the law into her own hands."

Virgie ran a hand through her hair. "Truth is stranger than fiction."

"Did you talk to her daughter?" Phyl asked.

"Yes. They were estranged for a good ten years. She said her mother's behavior had become irrational after the shooting in the café." The detective took a sip of wine and then asked, "How's the book coming along?"

"I'm working on the final revisions. The editor is foaming at the mouth to get her hands on it."

"What's the title?"

Phyl smiled. "*Murder on Castaway Island.*"

Acknowledgments

I'm hesitant to start thanking people because I'm sure to leave somebody out, but here goes. Bella Books: Linda Hill, thank you for letting me pitch my book to you at the GCLS con in Albuquerque. I was so nervous, and you were so kind and patient. Jessica Hill and everyone who had anything to do with getting this book published, thank you, thank you, thank you.

My colleague, English Professor Christina Lynch, at College of the Sequoias, thank you for the pre-NaNoWriMo workshop in 2018 and for inviting me to take her creative writing class the following semester. Those two things got this ball rolling.

My original Beta readers, Donna Bailey, Susan Allen, Erin Poole, and Toni Nikka, your feedback was much appreciated. Special thanks to my professional Beta/copyeditors Doreen Howard, Jazzy Mitchell, Lynette Beers, and Lara Zielinsky. Thank you all for donating your time and talents to the Golden Crown Literary Society auction. I definitely benefitted.

My editor, Ann Roberts. Thank you for your expert guidance and feedback. I couldn't have asked for a better editor.

And most importantly, my wife, Donna. Thank you for always saying yes. Every time I said I wanted to do something new: get a master's degree, start teaching part-time, quit my job and teach full-time, learn to play the flute, play in the college band, learn to play the ukulele, get a creative writing certificate, write a novel, marry me, and a dozen other things, she said yes, every single time.

About the Author

Alicia Gael (she/her) earned a Creative Writing Certificate from UC San Diego Extension, a Master's in Criminology from CSU Fresno, and is a graduate of the Golden Crown Literary Society Writing Academy. She is a retired probation officer and criminal justice professor. Her short stories have been published in *The Bangalore Review* (*Deception*) and *The Quiet Reader* (*No Time For Stories*). The first chapter of her yet-to-be-finished historical fiction novel, *The Journey*, was published in the 2022 CA Writer's Literary Review anthology.

When not writing, she can be found wine tasting, reading, playing the ukulele, or kayaking. She lives near the California central coast with her wife, Donna.

Alicia loves to hear from readers. You can follow her at:
Facebook: aliciagaelwrites
Instagram: aliciagael_writes
Bluesky: aliciagael.bsky.social
TikTok: @aliciagaelwrites
Sign up for her newsletter at www.aliciagael.com

More Titles from Bella Books